THE FAIRY WORLD IS WAITING....

★ "Beautiful bookmaking, lovely storytelling and wondrous illustrations...Readers will be enchanted." —*Kirkus Reviews*, starred review

★ "The lyrical narrative blends a contemporary setting with a fairy tale that might have been plucked from a distinctly different time and place." —*Publishers Weekly*, starred review

★ "[A] delicious companion novel." —*School Library Journal*, starred review

"There is an elegance and thoughtfulness to both the text and accompanying illustrations....Folktale and fairy tale fans who are seeking a longer adventure into which to settle will find this a perfect fit."
—*The Bulletin*

Praise for *The Cats of Tanglewood Forest*

A 2013 *NEW YORK TIMES* NOTABLE CHILDREN'S BOOK
A *NEW YORK TIMES* EDITORS' CHOICE BOOK
A SPRING 2013 KIDS' INDIE NEXT PICK
A SPRING 2013 PARENTS' CHOICE AWARDS APPROVED BOOK

"Thoroughly delightful...Lillian Kindred is a first-rate heroine, brave and bright and kind....Bewitching and wonderful."
—*The New York Times Book Review*

★ "De Lint zestfully combines the traditional and the original, the light and the dark, while Vess's luminous full-color illustrations, simultaneously fluid and precise, capture Lillian's effervescent blend of determination and curiosity." —*Publishers Weekly*, starred review

★ "Has a wonderfully old-fashioned fable-like feel to it, imparting a message of 'be careful what you wish for' through beautifully descriptive, finely tuned prose that leaves no doubt about the lesson being taught, yet makes the learning of it a joy." —*Quill & Quire*, starred review

"Sweetly magical...A satisfyingly folkloric, old-fashioned–feeling fable." —*Kirkus Reviews*

"Well suited as a charming read-aloud...The pencil and colored ink illustrations are lush and evocative." —*School Library Journal*

"The story's lyrical, folkloric style is well suited to a tale of magic and mystery." —*Booklist*

"A woodsy-wild adventure drenched in folklore magic...A new, original folktale that reads like a perennial favorite—a story passed down through generations after supper, at bedtime, or around a roaring fire. De Lint's storytelling is masterful and timeless."
—Ingrid Law, *New York Times* bestselling author of
the Newbery Honor Book *Savvy*

"A delicious and delightful book, with the feel of a beloved classic, by two of the world's finest fantasists."
—Holly Black, Newbery Honor author of *Doll Bones*

"[A] timeless tangled tale of magic and consequence, beautifully illuminated with the lush illustrations of Charles Vess. This is my new favorite feline folktale."
—Tony DiTerlizzi, *New York Times* bestselling author and
illustrator of The Spiderwick Chronicles

"An enchanted and enchanting journey that explores the strength of family ties, illuminated by Charles Vess's magical and haunting illustrations." —Franny Billingsley, author of *The Folk Keeper* and *Chime*

Seven Wild Sisters

A MODERN FAIRY TALE

Written by Charles de Lint ❧ Illustrated by Charles Vess

LITTLE, BROWN AND COMPANY

New York   Boston

Text copyright © 2014 by Charles de Lint
Illustrations copyright © 2014 by Charles Vess

Little, Brown and Company

Hachette Book Group
1290 Avenue of the Americas, New York, NY 10104
Visit us at lb-kids.com

Little, Brown and Company is a division of Hachette Book Group, Inc.
The Little, Brown name and logo are trademarks of Hachette Book Group, Inc.

The publisher is not responsible for websites (or their content) that are not owned by the publisher.

First Paperback Edition: July 2015
First published in hardcover in February 2014 by Little, Brown an Company
Seven Wild Sisters first appeared as a limited edition book written by Charles de Lint and illustrated by Charles Vess and was published in 2002 by Subterranean Press.

Library of Congress Cataloging-in-Publication Data
De Lint, Charles, 1951–
Seven wild sisters / written by Charles de Lint ; illustrated by Charles Vess.—First edition.
pages cm
"Seven Wild Sisters first appeared as a limited edition book written by Charles de Lint and illustrated by Charles Vess and was published in 2002 by Subterranean Press."
Summary: Sarah Jane Dillard discovers and helps an injured 'sangman fairy in the Tanglewood Forest, putting herself, her six sisters, and friends Aunt Lillian and the Apple Tree Man in the middle of a fairy feud.
ISBN 978-0-316-05356-3 (hc)—ISBN 978-0-316-05352-5 (pb)
[1. Adventure and adventurers—Fiction. 2. Fairies—Fiction. 3. Sisters—Fiction. 4. Magic—Fiction. 5. Kidnapping—Fiction.] I. Vess, Charles, illustrator. II. Title.
PZ7.D383857Sev 2013
[Fic]—dc23

2012045328

10 9 8 7 6 5 4 3 2 1

SC

Printed in China
Book design by Saho Fujii

Still for the red rock girls,
Anna Annabelle and Her Julieness,
but also for Nora:
May she find her own joys
up in those red rocks.

—*Charles de Lint*

For the rolling hills of southwestern Virginia
that I see right outside my studio window, where
stories like this one happen every single day.

—*Charles Vess*

"It's a long lane that never has no turns."

—*Arie Carpenter*

Spirits in the Woods

*T*here's those that call it ginseng, but 'round here we just call it 'sang. Don't know which is right. All I know for sure is that bees and 'sang don't mix, leastways not in these hills.

Their rivalry's got something to do with sweetness and light and wildflower pollen set against dark rooty things that live deep in the forest dirt. That's why bee spirits'll lead the 'sang poachers to those hidden 'sang beds. It's an unkindness you'd expect more from the Mean Fairy—you know, the way he shows up at parties after the work's all done.

'Course there's spirits in the hills. How could there not be? You think we're alone in this world? We have us a very peopled woods, and I've seen all kinds in my time, big and small.

The Father of Cats haunts these hills. Most times he's this big old panther, sleek and black, but the Kickaha say he can look like a handsome, black-haired man, the fancy takes him. I only ever saw him as a panther. Seeing yourself a panther is unusual enough, though I suppose it's something anybody who spends enough time in these woods can eventually claim. But I heard him talk.

Don't you smile. I don't tell lies.

Then there's the Green Boy—you want to watch out for him. He lives in the branches of trees and he's got him this great big smile because he's everybody's friend, that's a certain fact. He loves company, loves to joke and tell stories, but one day with him is like a year for everybody else you left behind.

See, some places, you've got to be careful on how the time passes. There's caves 'round these parts that can take you right out of this world and into another, but the days go by slower there, like they did for Rip Van Winkle. I met an artist once, he was gone twenty years in this world, but only a few days had passed for him on the other side.

What happened? He went back. That's another caution you need to heed. Places like that can take a powerful hold of you, make you feel like everything in your life is empty because you're not breathing magic.

There's wonders, no question, but there's danger, too, and that's not the only one. You listen to what I'm telling you.

Old Bubba's been seen more than once in these parts, but you stay clear of him. I know there's some have claimed they got the better of that old devil man, but if you bargain with him, I believe you'll carry a piece of his darkness inside you way into forever, doesn't matter that you got the best of him once.

I suppose the one I know best is the Apple Tree Man, lives in the oldest tree of the orchard. Do you know that old song?

> Jimmy had a penny,
> he put it in a can.
> He give it to the night
> and the Apple Tree Man.
> Singing, pour me a cider,
> like I never had me one.
> Pour me a cider,
> give everybody some.

I've known him since I was younger than you, but he hasn't changed much in all those years. He's still the same wrinkled, gnarly old fellow he was the first time I met him. The time is right, maybe I'll introduce the two of you.

Fairies? Oh, I've seen them, all right. Not every day, but they're out there.

First time, I was just a little girl. They were these little fox fire lights, dancing out there in the field like flickerbugs. It wasn't any snakebit fever that let me see them, though I did have the venom in me from a bite I got earlier that day. I could have died, lit a shuck right out of this world and there's me, no more than twelve years old, but the Apple Tree Man drew the poison right out of me with a madstone soaked in milk.

Him and the Father of Cats, they saved my life, though only the Father of Cats wanted payment, so I owe him a favor. If I can't pay it when he comes asking, then one of my descendants has to. Trouble is, I never had any children. I'm the last of this line of Kindreds, so far as I know.

Anywise, instead of dying, I got me a big piece of magic that night. It was hard to hang on to for a time, but I know no matter what else I experience in this world, scraps and pieces of that magic'll be with me forever. I don't question that.

You get on in years and it can be hard for a body to tell a difference between things that happened and things you thought might have happened, but I know better. There's a veil, thin as a funeral shroud, that divides this world from some other. You do it right and you can walk on either side of it. The world you find on one side or the other, the people you meet, they're all real.

I reckon it's been seventy years, maybe longer, since the Father of Cats came out of the forest and made me beholden to him. I'm getting on now. I'm not saying my time is come, but it's getting there. Year by year. And I guess I'd just like to see him again. Pay my debt before it's time for me to move on.

arah Jane Dillard didn't think the old woman was crazy, though most everybody else did. Folks liked her well enough—they'd pass the time with her when she came into town and all—but what else could you think about a woman in her eighties, living alone on a mountaintop, an hour's walk in from the county road?

It wasn't like she was a granny woman who needed her solitude. She had her herbs and simples, and she'd be the first to lend a hand, somebody needed help, but she wasn't known in these parts for cures and midwifery like the Welch women were. She was just an old woman, kept herself to herself. Not unfriendly, but not looking to step into social circles anytime soon, either.

"What does she *do* up there, all on her own?" someone or other would ask from time to time.

They might not know, but Sarah Jane did.

Aunt Lillian lived the same now as she had since she was a child. She had no phone, no electricity, no running water. The only food she bought was what she couldn't grow herself or gather from the woods around her.

So most of her time was taken up with the basic tasks of eking out a living from her land and the forest. It took a lot of hours in a day to see after her gardens, the cow and chickens, the orchard and hives. To go into the woods in season to gather greens and herbs, nuts and berries, and 'sang. Water had to be carried in from the springhouse, the woodbox filled, and any number of other day-to-day chores needed doing.

It wasn't so much a question of what she did, as there hardly being the time in a day to get it all done.

"But don't you find it hard?" Sarah Jane had asked her once. "Keeping up with it all?"

Aunt Lillian had smiled. "Hard's being confined to a sickbed, like some my age are," she'd said. "Hard's not being able to look after yourself. What I do…it's just living, girl."

"But you could buy your food instead of growing it."

"Sure, I could, except it wouldn't necessarily be as pleasing to my soul."

"You find weeding a garden pleasing?"

"You should try it, girl. You might be surprised."

The trail to Aunt Lillian's house started in the pasture beside the Welches' farm, then took a winding route up into the hills, traveling alongside the creek as it flowed down the length of the hollow.

In spring the creek grew swollen, the water tumbling over stone staircases, overflowing pools, and running quickly along the narrows until it finally reached the pasture, where it dove under the county road before continuing on its way. By fall the creek was reduced to a trickle, though it never dried up completely. There were always a few deep pools, even in the hottest months of the summer, home to fish,

spring peepers, and deep-throated bullfrogs, and perfect for a cool dip on a sweltering day.

Tall sprucy-pine grew on either side of the trail, sharing the steep slopes of the hollow with yellow birch, oak, and beech. Under them was a thick shrub layer of rhododendrons and mountain laurel. Higher up, tulip trees and more sprucy-pine rose on either side with a thick understory of redbud, magnolia, and dogwood. Even with her yellow hound, Root, at her side, Sarah Jane had seen deer, fox, hares, raccoons, and possum, not to mention the endless chorus of birds and squirrels scolding all intruders from the safety of the trees—when they weren't occupied with their own business, that is.

The walk through these woods, with the conversation of the creek as constant company, was something Sarah Jane quickly grew to love. It didn't matter if she was just ambling along with Root, or pulling Aunt Lillian's cart—fetching the supplies that were dropped off for Aunt Lillian at the Welches' farm or hauling them back to her old house up in the hills.

Sarah Jane's own family lived next door to the Welches, on what everybody still called the old Shaffer farm. Though they'd been living there for the better part of ten years now, and her grandparents for five years before that, she'd become resigned to knowing that it would probably never be called the Dillard farm.

They'd moved here from Hazard after her father died—she, her mother, and her six sisters—to live with Granny Burrell, her maternal grandmother. The Burrells had bought the farm from the Shaffers a few years before Sarah Jane's family arrived and hadn't had any more luck losing the Shaffer name than they did. When Granny Burrell died, she left the farm to Sarah Jane's mother and now it was home to their little clan of red-haired, independent-thinking girls.

"If you weren't so bullish," Granny Burrell would say, "you'd have better luck getting another father for those wayward girls of yours."

"Maybe they don't want another father," Sherry Dillard would tell her mother. "And I sure plan to be choosy about the next man I have in my life. I'd just as soon have none than get me one that won't match up to my Jimmy."

"You're going to ruin your life."

"Least it's *my* life," their mother would say.

But if their mother had a mind of her own, her

daughters gave a whole new meaning to independent thinking.

Adie, named after their paternal grandmother, Ada, was the eldest. From the time she could walk, she'd always been in one kind of trouble or another, from sassing the teachers in grade school to eloping at sixteen with Johnny Garland, the two of them high-tailing it out of the county on Johnny's motorcycle. She came back seven months later, unrepentant, but done with boyfriends for the time being.

The twins, Laurel and Bess, were born the year after her. They were also mad about boys, but their first love was music—making it, dancing to it, anything there might be that had to do with it. They both sang, making those sweet harmonies that only sisters can. Laurel played the fiddle, Bess the banjo, and the two could be found at any barn dance or hooley within a few miles' radius of the farm, kicking up their heels on the dance floor with an ever-rotating cast of partners, or playing their instruments on the stage, keeping up with the best of them. When they were home, just the two of them, they'd amuse themselves arranging pop music from the seventies and eighties into old-timey and bluegrass settings.

Sarah Jane was born two years after the twins. She was the middle child, double-named because this time her mother meant to be ready if she had another set of twins. They'd be Sarah and Jane if they were girls, Robert and William if they were boys. When she got just the one girl, she couldn't decide which of the two girl names to pick, so she gave her both.

As the middle child, Sarah Jane bridged her sisters not only in years, but also in temperament. Like her older sisters, she loved to dance and run a little wild. But she also loved reading and drawing, and could sit quietly with her younger sister Elsie for hours, watching the light change on the underwater stones as the creek streamed above them or contemplating the possibility that what the crows rasped and cawed at each other might actually be some secret language that people didn't understand.

Elsie was different from her sisters in other ways. She was lean and wiry, the quietest of the girls, more so since they'd moved here. Now she spent all her time in the surrounding woods and hills, stalking anything and everything, from bugs and birds to fox and deer.

Their mother jokingly referred to Elsie as her

feral daughter and that wasn't far off the mark. Elsie was always happiest out in the woods, day or night, and no matter what the season. She could run as fast as a deer, but she could be almost preternaturally still, too. Sarah Jane had never known anyone who could sit so quietly for so long. "I'm just watching the grass grow," Elsie would say when she was found in a meadow, gazing off across the wildflowers and weeds.

And finally there were Ruth and Grace, also twins. They'd belied the biblical ring of their names from the moment they came home from the hospital, working like a tag team as they ensured that if they couldn't get a full night's sleep for their first two years in the world, then no one else in the household would, either. No sooner would one drop off than the other would start in crying, and there would be two fussing infants to be dealt with once more.

The older they grew, the more of a handful they became. They could never simply do a thing without first knowing the how and why of its needing to be done, and that knowing had to be explained in great and painstaking detail. But it was better to take the time to explain, else they could take a thing apart just to see how it worked, and it might never get put back together again.

They loved playing practical jokes, though never mean-spirited ones. And stubborn? A mule was a pushover compared to trying to shift them once they had their minds set on a thing.

⌒

Sarah Jane had known for years that an old woman lived at the end of the trail that began in the Welches' pasture. She'd even seen her a few times, if only from a distance, which suited Sarah Jane just fine. Adie and the older twins were forever spooking the younger girls, telling them that if they weren't good, the old witch woman who lived in the hills would come and get them. She had this oven, see, big enough to hold a child trussed up like a roasting chicken....

For ages Sarah Jane and her younger sisters had lived in fear of her. But one summer, three years ago, Sarah Jane and Elsie had dared each other to follow the trail to see where the old woman lived.

They took Root with them. That yellow short-haired hound of Sarah Jane's was a couple of years old at the time and full of beans, forever digging in the garden or wherever else he thought he might find a bone or a rabbit burrow, though Mama swore that he didn't need an excuse. Root was just a dog that was happy digging.

"It's your own fault," she'd tell Sarah Jane. "Giving him such a name."

How she got that dog was a whole other story, in and of itself.

Sarah Jane was lying abed one night watching moon shadows of beech trees outside as they moved and stretched across the ceiling of her room. For some odd reason, she hadn't been able to sleep. Her head was filled with everything and nothing—a fairly common occurrence, really.

She heard the dog start to cry an hour or so after midnight—a distant whining that occasionally broke into louder yelping. At first she thought that one of the neighbors had gotten a new pet and put it out on a chain for its first night out. There was that desperation in its voice that dogs do so well—an anxiety that can make you believe the theory that dogs live entirely in the present, with no recollection of the past or hope for the future. This dog had been put out and, so far as it could see, that was where it had to be for the rest of its life.

But as she lay there, alternately dozing and waking up when the cries got louder, she got to thinking about what if the dog was really in trouble. It might have broken loose from somewhere and gotten its chain wrapped around a tree or something. That had happened before and not so far from here. She'd overheard George Welch telling her mother about finding the bones of a dog one spring, how it had still been wearing a collar, its lead entangled in the roots of a tree.

"That was a hard death," she remembered him saying. "I wouldn't wish it on anyone, man or critter."

Sighing, she threw back the comforter and sat up. The floor was icy on her bare feet as she padded across the room to where she'd draped her clothes over a chair. Elsie began to stir as Sarah Jane was getting dressed.

"Whatcha...doing...?" Elsie asked, her voice thick with sleep.

"Nothing," Sarah Jane told her. "I'm just going to get a little air."

"But...it's the middle of the night...." Elsie murmured.

Like she herself hadn't been out and about in the woods in the middle of the night a hundred times before, looking for owls and bats and who knew what.

"Go back to sleep," Sarah Jane said.

She thought Elsie might protest—after all, this was a midnight excursion into her beloved woods—but she'd already fallen back to sleep before Sarah Jane finished dressing and left the room.

Downstairs she put some biscuits in her pocket, got a length of rope from the shed, and went out into the fall night with a lantern that she didn't bother to light. The moonlight was enough. Once she'd closed the door behind her, she stood quietly for a long moment and tilted her face up to the sky, drinking in the stars, the dark, and the wind.

Then she heard the dog yelp again.

It took her a moment to decide where the sound was coming from—it was always tricky with a wind—then she started across the back fields, going right up the mountain and into the edge of Tanglewood Forest.

It didn't take her long to find the dog, trapped as it was. He had a rope around his neck, the loose end of which had gotten caught in some old barbed wire.

By the time she reached him, he was so entangled that his head was pressed right against the old fencepost. A barb from the wire was pricking him just above his eye and there was blood on his fur.

She approached quietly, speaking in a low and comforting voice. When she was close enough, she put out her hand so that he could smell her. She wasn't exactly nervous, but you never could tell with dogs in a pickle. When he thumped his tail and gave her hand a little lick, she gave up all caution.

He lay still while she worked the rope loose, wishing she'd brought a knife. Before she had him completely free, she made a slip knot with the rope she'd brought and looped it around his neck. When she got the last of the old rope untangled, the dog stood up on trembling legs and leaned against her. He gazed up at her, his eyes big in the moonlight.

"Now who do you belong to?" she asked, ruffling the short hair between his ears.

He grinned and bumped his head against her, tail wagging furiously. She smiled and brought him home, taking him right up into her room. After the night he'd had, she couldn't bear the idea of tying him up outside or locking him in the shed. He lay

down on the floor beside her bed, but as soon as she got under the covers, he was up on the bed with her, stretched out along her side.

Mama was going to kill her, she remembered thinking before she fell asleep with her hand on his chest.

When she woke, he was lying on the floor again, and that was how Mama found them. She always felt that he'd done that on purpose, just to get on Mama's good side. And it had worked, once Sarah Jane told her story.

"You can keep him till we find who he belongs to," Mama said.

"Maybe we never will," Elsie said, her face hopeful.

All her sisters had immediately fallen in love with him.

"A dog that good-natured has to have someone who loves him," Mama replied.

"He does," Sarah Jane said. "He has us."

"You know what I mean."

Sarah Jane nodded.

But no one knew whose he was. No one came to claim him. And by the time the snows came, he and Sarah Jane had become inseparable. He couldn't go to school with her, but wherever else she went, he was usually somewhere nearby. And best of all, he'd made Mama feel safer about when she or Elsie went wandering in the woods, like they were doing now.

So with Root ranging ahead of them on the trail or crashing through the underbrush on one side or the other, the two girls followed the well-worn path into the hills, walking arm in arm.

Sarah Jane felt brave enough with the company. But then Root took off and, halfway to the old woman's cabin, Elsie got intrigued by a hornets' nest and insisted on studying it for a time. Sarah Jane had been scared of bees and hornets ever since a classmate of hers got stung to death last summer. It was an allergic reaction, she'd heard at the funeral, but she couldn't shake the thought that it could happen to anybody—like getting bit by a snake. So the last thing she wanted to do was stand around looking at that great big papery gray nest hanging from the branch of a small laurel. And that was the thing—how could such a slender branch support such a big nest anyway? There was just something not right about it.

"Come on, Elsie," she said. "What happened to our adventure?"

"I need to study this," Elsie said.

Her voice was distracted and Sarah Jane could tell that she was already in what Adie called full Indian scout mode. When she got like this, you could set off a firecracker under her feet and she wouldn't notice.

"You go on ahead. I'll catch up," Elsie added.

Go on by herself?

Sarah Jane looked up the trail. The sun was breaking through the trees in cathedraling beams and it was pretty as all get-out, but looks could be deceiving. Especially when you knew the trail ended at a witch's house. Except she didn't have to actually talk to the witch, she reminded herself. She could just go close enough to have a peek at her house and then come back. That wouldn't be so hard. And it sure beat staring at that wasps' nest, waiting to get stung.

So on she went, but more slowly now, because nothing felt quite the same anymore. It might only have been her imagination, but the shafts of sunlight didn't seem to penetrate the canopy as brightly as they had before, and the woods felt darker. The sound of the squirrels as they rustled through the leaves was magnified, so that she thought she heard much larger shapes moving about, just out of sight. Bears. Panthers. Wolves.

Her heart beat far too quickly.

Stop it, she thought. You're just scaring yourself.

She looked back and there was Elsie, still scrunched up in the small space between a bush and a hemlock, happily contemplating the wasps' nest, oblivious to any danger, either from wasps or whatever else might be in the woods, hungry to have itself a bite of her.

I'm not scared of these woods, Sarah Jane thought, trying to convince herself that she actually believed it. There was nothing here that was going to hurt her so long as she kept out of its way, and that included witches. She could go and spy on her just like Elsie was spying on those wasps. It was a time to be cautious, yes. But not scared.

So she squared her shoulders and set off again, whistling for Root. She wasn't ready to admit it just then, having already convinced herself that she could be brave all on her own, but she felt a great sense of relief when the dog came bounding down the hillside and skidded to a stop beside her. He mooshed his head against her leg, tongue lolling, gaze turned up to her face and plainly asking, "Where are my pats?"

"Yes, yes," she told him as she ruffled his short fur with both her hands. "You're my good boy."

Dog at her heel, she proceeded along the path, giving Root a soft call back every time he looked to go off exploring. And that was how she finally crept up on Aunt Lillian's homestead, back in the hills.

Aunt Lillian wasn't doing any sort of witchy things when Sarah Jane finally left the path and crept through the bushes to spy on her. Not unless tending garden had some witchy significance that Sarah Jane didn't know anything about. In fact, nothing about the old woman's homestead seemed to have anything to do with the grisly business of being a witch—or at least Sarah Jane's imagining of what a witch would be like and where she'd live.

There was no aura of evil and dread. No children's bones dangling from the trees. No strange and noxious liquids bubbling in cauldrons—unless those were hidden in the house. No capering goblins or familiars or other unholy consorts.

With a warning hand on Root's head to keep him quiet, she settled down in the bushes and studied the old woman's homestead. Closest to her was the garden where Aunt Lillian was weeding her vegetables, using a hoe that was no different from the one Sarah Jane used on their own garden back home. To the right, rising up the slope, was an apple orchard and several beehives. A clapboard house with a tin roof, corn crib, and front porch stood on the far side of the garden, surrounded by the usual gaggle of hangers-on: a woodpile, a chicken house, a smoking shed, a springhouse, and various storage sheds. On the far side of the house and a little to the left, she could make out the roof of a small barn and what looked to be a cornfield, the young stalks no more than a foot high at the moment. The woods pressed close on the far side of the barn and along the edges of the orchard.

It all looked so normal. Just as the old woman did, hoeing her garden.

Sarah Jane was so caught up on trying to find some hidden, shadowy meaning to Aunt Lillian's work, that when the old woman suddenly started to speak, she thought her heart would simply stop in her chest. The old woman didn't look directly at her, but it soon became obvious that she knew Sarah Jane was there.

"Now the way I see it," Aunt Lillian said, "there are only two reasons a body would hide in the bushes to spy on someone. Either they mean them harm, or they're too shy to say hello hello, so they skulk around in the bushes instead. I wonder which you are, girl."

Sarah Jane held herself more still than she ever had before, her fingers tightening their pressure on Root's head until he began to squirm a little. But it was no use. The old woman knew she was there as surely as Sarah Jane's mother could spot a lie. She wasn't even looking in Sarah Jane's direction, but it was plain as plain could be who she was talking to.

"'Course I'm hoping you're just shy," Aunt Lillian went on, "as I wouldn't be minding me someone to talk to every once in a while. I'm not saying I get lonely, living up here on my ownsome, but everybody enjoys a spot of company—maybe a lending hand with a strong, young back to put behind it."

She didn't sound so awful, Sarah Jane thought. She didn't sound like her older sisters' stories at all.

Swallowing her fear, Sarah Jane slowly rose from the bushes. She and the old woman looked at each other for a long moment, the woman patient, Sarah Jane not sure what she should say or do. Root broke the silence. Freed of Sarah Jane's hand, he bounded out of the bushes.

"Shoo!" Aunt Lillian said. "Get out of my greens, you big lug!"

To Sarah Jane's surprise, Root stopped dead in his tracks and carefully backed out of the garden.

"How'd you do that?" she asked. "It takes me forever just to get his attention long enough to make him stop digging or whatever."

The answer came to her even while she was speaking: magic. The old lady *was* a witch woman. Of course she could make an animal do whatever she wanted it to.

She wished she'd never asked the question, but Aunt Lillian only smiled.

"He has to know you mean business," she said. "That's all. Dog's like a fella. He doesn't think you're serious, he'll just carry right on with whatever mischief

he's getting himself into." She cocked her head and winked. "'Course you've still got a few years to go before you need to be worrying about fellas. You want some lemonade, girl?"

"Sure. My name's Sarah Jane."

"I'm guessing you'll be one of the Dillard girls— the ones living on the old Shaffer farm."

Sarah Jane shook her head. "No, it's the Dillard farm," she tried.

Aunt Lillian smiled again. "I'm Lily Kindred, but everybody calls me Aunt Lillian."

"Why do they do that?"

"Same reason some folks ask a lot of questions, I guess, and that's a different reason for each person. Now how about that lemonade?"

Sarah Jane followed the old woman back to her house. She sat on the steps of the porch with Root while Aunt Lillian went inside. Though the house it- self was shaded by a beech tree on one side and a pair of old oaks on the other, there were no trees grow- ing on the side where she was sitting. She had a fine view of the meadows that ran down the slope to the creek and watched a handful of crows playing in the air, dive-bombing each other like planes in an old war movie, until Aunt Lillian returned with a glass pitcher of lemonade. Ice clinked against the sides as she poured them each a tall glass.

"The ice house needs replenishing," Aunt Lillian said as she sat down beside Sarah Jane. "Reckon it's time to take a walk into town and make me a few orders."

"You really live out here all alone?"

"I do now. Used to live here with my aunt, but she passed away some time ago, God rest her soul."

"Without running water or TV or anything?"

"Without anything? Girl, I've got the whole of the Lord's creation right at my front door."

"You know what I mean."

Aunt Lillian nodded. "I'm happy out here. It's where I've lived the most of my life. It's not so easy now as it was when I was younger, but I get help. Folks in town will help pack my goods up the trail and there's a fella lives deeper in the woods comes by from time to time to help me with the heavy work."

Sarah Jane couldn't imagine it.

"And what about you, girl?" Aunt Lillian said. "What brings you so far from home?"

Sarah Jane sighed.

"I guess you just forgot," she said. "My name's Sarah Jane."

She hoped she didn't sound impolite, but the way the woman kept referring to her as "girl" felt too much like someone talking about their dog or a cat.

"I didn't forget," Aunt Lillian said. "I may be a lot of things, but forgetful isn't one of them. I just don't like to be using a body's name too often. You never know who or what might be listening in."

That was when she first began to tell Sarah Jane her stories about the Apple Tree Man and the other magical creatures that peopled these hills.

CHAPTER TWO

o, while Aunt Lillian wasn't really Sarah Jane's aunt, she as much became the one that Sarah Jane didn't have. After that first meeting, Sarah Jane was a regular visitor to the Kindred homestead, sometimes with one or more of her sisters in tow, but usually it was just Root and her. The old woman was happy for the company and Mama didn't seem to mind Sarah Jane neglecting some of her chores at home because she worked twice as hard for Aunt Lillian.

"She's being a good neighbor," Mama had said one time when Laurel complained that, as far as she was concerned, the rest of them were doing far too many of what were supposed to be Sarah Jane's chores. "We should all be so lucky to have someone help us out when we get to Lillian Kindred's age."

But chores didn't seem like work around Aunt Lillian. There was so much to learn—things that Sarah Jane had never even realized a curiosity about before, because there was so much about her life that she'd always taken for granted.

You needed milk or eggs or butter? She'd always gone to the supermarket. But with Aunt Lillian you had to milk the cow, churn the butter, chase down the secret nests of the hens to find their eggs.

In the Dillard household you simply put something in the fridge to keep it cold. Aunt Lillian had an ice house that was as easy to use in the winter, but come summer you had to haul in the ice from where it was dropped off for her at the Welch farm, chipping pieces off to make ice cubes for their tea.

You didn't turn on the stove to cook. Before you could put on a single pot, you chopped wood, laid a fire in the big cast-iron stove in the kitchen, started it up, and waited for the heat to build.

Honey came fresh from a comb rather than a jar, though that was something Sarah Jane let Aunt Lillian harvest on her own. "You don't have to worry about my bees," Aunt Lillian assured a skeptical Sarah Jane. "I gift the spirits connected to them, so they don't sting me. It's the wild ones you need to be careful of."

Soap started by making lye—pouring water over the fireplace ashes in the ash hopper, the resulting liquid caught in an old kettle. When there was enough lye for a run of soap, it was brought to a boil, dipping a chicken feather into the solution from time to time to see if it was ready. When the lye took the fuzz off the stem of the feather, it was strong enough to make soap. At that point Aunt Lillian added fat that the Welches had saved for her from when they killed their hogs. The lye would eventually eat the fat and become a thick brown soap.

Aunt Lillian didn't take vitamins. Instead she made a tonic with a recipe that included ratsbane, bark from the yellow poplar, red dogwood and wild cherry, the roots of burdock, yellow dock, and sarsaparilla. She boiled it all in water until the result was thick and black, then bottled it with enough whiskey added to keep it from spoiling. It tasted terrible, but Aunt Lillian took a tablespoon every day and she was never sick.

And on and on it went. Every new revelation gave Sarah Jane a deeper appreciation for all the necessities that she'd simply taken for granted before this. And then there was the satisfaction of knowing that they had this bounty from work they'd done themselves.

Food was what really stood out in Sarah Jane's mind. Everything tasted so much better. The ice cream they made in summer was thick and creamy, bursting with flavor. Biscuits, breads, fried pies. Stews, soups, salads. Everything.

"That's because you're making it from the ground up," Aunt Lillian told her. "You know every moment of that plant's life, from when you put the seed in the dirt to its sitting on the table in front of you. It's like eating with family instead of strangers."

Sarah Jane couldn't explain to her sisters why it seemed like such a better way to live. She couldn't even remember how she'd once been as incredulous as they were now that Aunt Lillian could simply ignore a hundred years of progress, which, for most, made the business of living so much easier. All she could say was that she liked to do things Aunt Lillian's way. She finally understood what the term "an honest day's work" meant because, after an afternoon tending to the animals and working in the garden, she just felt "righteously tired," as Aunt Lillian would put it. She would return home with a spring in her step, never mind the long day she'd put in.

And then there were the stories.

The stories.

Sarah Jane loved them all. It didn't matter if it was the simple history of some herb they were out looking for in the woods, the offhand explanation of why a strip of white cloth tied to a stake kept deer out of the garden, or the strange and tangled stories that centered on the magical neighbors who, Aunt Lillian assured her, lived in the woods all around them. It got so that Sarah Jane *expected* to see fairies, or the Father of Cats, or *some* magical being or other every time she made the trip through the woods to and from Aunt Lillian's homestead.

But she never did. Not even the Apple Tree Man.

"He's a shy old fellow," Aunt Lillian explained one day when they were sitting on the porch, shucking peas. "I left biscuits under his tree every morning for more years than I can remember before he finally stepped out of the bark one day to talk to me."

"Does he still visit you?"

The old woman shook her head. "Not so much these past few years. Time was, if I didn't talk to him every day, I'd at least see him crossing the meadow at dusk and we'd smile and wave to each other. But he's a funny old fellow. Gets all these notions in his head."

"Like what?" Sarah Jane wanted to know.

She was always full of questions when it came to Aunt Lillian's magical neighbors. The more she heard about them, the more she needed to know.

Aunt Lillian shrugged. "Oh, you know. 'Trouble's brewing' is a favorite of his, like there isn't always some sort of feud going on with the fairy folk. They can be as cantankerous as old Bill Widgins at the post office, ready to take offense at the slightest provocation."

"So do they fight each other?"

"You mean with sticks and little swords and the like?"

Sarah Jane nodded.

"I suppose they might, but I've never seen it. From what I can tell, mostly they play tricks on each other. I guess the longest-running feud in these hills

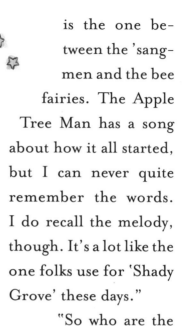

is the one between the 'sangmen and the bee fairies. The Apple Tree Man has a song about how it all started, but I can never quite remember the words. I do recall the melody, though. It's a lot like the one folks use for 'Shady Grove' these days."

"So who are the good guys?" Sarah Jane asked. "The 'sangmen or the bee fairies?"

Aunt Lillian laughed. "There's no real good or bad when it comes to fairies, girl. Not the way we think of it. They just are, and their disagreements can be pretty much incomprehensible to the likes of you and me. The only thing I do know for sure is not to get mixed up in the middle of it. That's the one sure road to trouble."

"I wouldn't," Sarah Jane assured her.

Easy to say, sitting on the porch the way they were, shaded from the afternoon sun, sharing a pleasant task with a friend. But quite another matter, alone in the dark in Tanglewood Forest, when the one sure thing, it seemed, was to choose a side or die.

Away

CHAPTER THREE

Sarah Jane

I was never much good in school. I don't know why. Grammar, math, geography—none of it meant all that much to me. I liked English for the stories, but I didn't take to all the rules about language. I liked history, too—more stories, only these were true—but I couldn't seem to care about what order they went in. Memorizing dates and names and such sure didn't seem to make them any better or worse than they already were.

I didn't know what I was ever going to do with my life. Laurel and Bess had their music. Elsie had her nature studies and art. The younger twins weren't of an age where it mattered much yet. That left only

Adie and me with our futures unaccounted for. I suppose you could say that Adie'd already taken on the role of the black sheep, though she hadn't done anything particularly colorful in months.

"I don't know what's going to come of you," Mama would say when I brought home another report card and none of it good.

I didn't, either. Leastways, not until I met Aunt Lillian, and you already know how that came about. But once I understood how there was another way a body could live than the one that seemed to lie afore me, well, I took to it like a kitten chasing a butterfly.

I guess my story really starts at 'sang harvest time, the third year after I met Aunt Lillian, and maybe I should have started there. Miss Cook, my English composition teacher, says that's the way to do it. You start when the story's already under way and fit in whatever background you find yourself needing as you go along.

But I don't think that way. I like to know the long history of a thing, not just where and what it might be now, and since this is my story, I suppose I can tell it any way I like. It's not like Miss Cook's going to mark me on it.

The beginning of September is the start of 'sang season, running through to the first frost. 'Sang's one of the few things Aunt Lillian takes out of the ground that she didn't put in herself, and it's pretty much the only thing she takes to market. Most anything she needs she can grow or collect in the hills around her home, but she needs a little cash for the few items she can't, and that's where the 'sang comes in.

She never takes much, just enough for her own

needs and for the few extra dollars she spends in town. I asked her about that the first time we went harvesting, me trailing after her like the big-footed, clumsy town girl I was, her walking with the grace and quiet of a cat, though she was at least five times my age. And she seemed tireless, too. Like her old bones didn't know the meaning of being old.

I learned to walk like her. I learned pretty much everything I know from her.

"It doesn't pay to be greedy," she told me. "Truth is, I feel a little bad as it is, taking more than I need to pay my bills, but if I wasn't selling 'sang, I'd still be selling something, and the 'sang and me, we've come to an agreement about all of this."

I was kind of surprised when she let me go on my own that morning. It was the first time I can remember that she'd begged off on a ramble. She didn't come right out and say she was feeling too old—"Got a mess of chores to do this morning. You go on ahead, girl"—but I knew that's what it was and my heart near broke. Still, I didn't say anything. Aunt Lillian was like us Dillard girls. She had her own mind about things and once it was made up, there was no shifting it. So I wasn't going to argue and say she wasn't too old. But I couldn't help remembering something Mama had said earlier in the summer.

"It makes you wonder," she'd said as we were sitting down to breakfast. "What's she going to do when she can't make it on her own anymore?"

"She's got me," I said.

"I know, sweetheart. But you've got a life to live, too. There's going to come a point when Lily Kindred's going to need full-time care and I hate to think of her in a state-run nursing home."

"She'd die first."

Mama didn't say anything. She just nodded, standing at the stove, her back to me. I didn't say anything about how I was planning to move up to Aunt Lillian's and live there full time once I was finished with school.

Anyway, I went out on my own that morning, leaving Root with Aunt Lillian. I love that dog, but all he's got to do is see me digging and he'd be right in there, helping me out, and two shakes of a stick later the whole patch'd be dug up, and that's not the way to do it.

I had a knapsack on my back and a walking stick in hand and I made good time through the woods, heading for the north slopes where the 'sang grows best under a thick canopy of poplar and beech, maple, dogwood, and oak. The ground's stony here and drains well, home to a whole mess of plants, each of them useful or just pretty. I smiled, thinking about that.

"That's got no use except to be pretty," Aunt Lillian had told me once when I'd asked about some flower we'd come upon during one of our rambles. Then she'd grinned. "Though I guess pretty's got its own use, seeing how it makes us feel so good just to look on it."

In season, these slopes are home to all the 'sang's companion plants. Blue cohosh, baneberry, and maidenhair fern. Jack-in-the-pulpit, yellow lady-slippers, and trilliums. Bloodroot, false Solomon's seal, and what some call the little brother of the 'sang: goldenseal. You find them and if the conditions are right, you could find yourself some 'sang.

Now there's a right and a wrong way to harvest 'sang.

The wrong way's to go in and just start in digging up plants with no never you mind. Stripping the area, or harvesting the first plants. You do any of that, it rankles the spirits, and when you come back, you won't find nothing growing but memories.

The right way's complicated, but it ensures that

the spirits understand your respect for them and the patch'll keep growing. You've got to come with humility in your heart and offer up prayers before you even start in considering to dig.

I remember thinking it was funny the first time I saw Aunt Lillian doing it, this old woman making her offerings of words and smoke and tobacco to invisible presences that I wasn't entirely convinced were even there. But then she had me do it with her, the two of us saying the words, waving our smudgesticks, laying our tobacco offerings on the ground as we went through it all, once for each of the four directions, and I'll be damned if I didn't feel something.

I can't explain exactly what. A stir in the air. A warm feeling in my chest. The sure knowing that we weren't alone in that old patch, that there were invisible presences all around us who accepted our offerings and, in return, would allow us to take some of the bounty of this place.

I looked at Aunt Lillian with big, wide eyes and she just grinned.

"Start in a-digging, girl," she said. "We've got our permission. Only mind you don't take a plant until it's at least six years old."

"How can you tell?"

You ever see 'sang growing in the wild? Ginseng, I guess some folks call it. It doesn't grow much above a foot, a foot and a half in these hills, and has a stiff stalk holding up a pair of leaves, each leaf divided in five like the fingers on your hand and looking a bit like those you'd find on a chestnut. The little cluster of yellow-green flowers turns to red berries that drop off around the end of August. It takes a couple of years to come up from seed, slow-growing and long-lived if left alone. The roots are what gets used for medicine, but there's some that use the leaves for tea.

"See these prongs?" Aunt Lillian asked me. "Where the leaves are growing?"

I nodded.

"You only want to dig these here, with four or five prongs. They stay at a two-prong for at least two or three years, then grow into a three-prong and finally a four, if they stand long enough. We don't want to take them too young. The roots won't be that big, you see? But if we leave them stand, we can harvest them in a year or two. This is an old patch that the poachers haven't found, so the ones we're going to take could be anywhere from six or seven years old to twenty-five."

"Where did you learn all of this?" I asked.

"Some I got from Aunt Em," she told me. "But most of this I learned from John Creek. That's his grandson Oliver I told you about before, camps up in the woods behind my place in the summer and comes down from time to time to lend me a hand with the heavy work when it's needed." She shook her head and smiled. "He was a busy man, John was. Had him sixteen daughters, plus another from his wife's first marriage."

I remember thinking then that I couldn't imagine sharing a bathroom with that many sisters, and nothing's changed since.

After harvesting, Aunt Lillian carefully washed those "green" roots and air-dried them under a shaded lean-to by the barn that she kept just for that purpose. It took maybe a month for them to dry. If you tried to heat them or dry them in the sun, they lost their potency. Once the roots were dried, Aunt Lillian boxed them up and took them into town to sell, though she always kept a few for her own tinctures and medicines.

When I got to the patch, I set down my walking stick and took off my knapsack. First thing I did was have me a long swallow of water, then I pulled out the things I'd need before I could start digging. It wasn't much. Smudgestick and matches. Dried tobacco leaves, rolled up and tied with red thread.

I was a little nervous, this being the first time I'd done this on my own, but by the time I was facing the last compass point, I was feeling not so much confidence, but at peace. Everything seemed real quiet in the woods around me and I could sense a pressure in the air, pushing at me. Not like a wind, more like the air was leaning against me on all sides.

I laid down the last of the tobacco and picked up the smudgestick. Waving it slowly back and forth in front of me, I spoke through the smoke, talking to the spirits, honoring them the way Aunt Lillian had taught me.

When I was done, I stuck the end of the smudgestick back into the ground and sat on my heels, drinking in the sensation that the prayers had left with me, this comforting feeling of being a part of something bigger than myself. I was still me, but whatever haunted this 'sang patch was letting me feel part of it as well.

Finally I reached over to my knapsack to get out the wooden trowel I'd brought.

And froze.

I hadn't given much consideration to the little pile of sticks and moss and leaves that I'd set my knapsack down beside. But the sticks were gone now and in their place was the strangest little creature I'd ever seen. It was a little man, I guess, if you can imagine a man that small, with roots for arms and legs, and mossy hair, skin brown as the dirt and wrinkled like cedar bark. He was maybe a foot tall, dressed in some kind of mottled green-and-brown shirt that looked like it was made of leaves and belted at the waist. His head was heart-shaped, his features all sharp edges and angles.

He made a little moan and I started, suddenly aware that I hadn't been breathing. His eyes fluttered open, then closed again, huge saucer-shaped eyes as dark as blackberries.

It was obvious that there was something wrong with him and it wasn't hard to see what. He looked like he'd lost an argument with a porcupine, as there were hundreds of quills sticking out of his skin. I leaned closer to look at them and realized they were arrows. Tiny arrows.

I looked quickly around, expecting at any minute

to be ambushed myself by a horde of miniature creatures with bows and arrows, but the 'sang patch was still. The little rootman and I had it to ourselves.

His eyes fluttered open again. This time they stayed open and I didn't flinch back.

"Are...are you okay?" I asked. Stupid question. Of course he wasn't okay. "Is there anything I can do to help you?"

"Arrows," he said.

His voice was husky and lower in timbre than I was expecting from a man the size of a small raccoon.

"Lots of them," I agreed.

"Need...out..."

I gave a slow nod. I could do that.

"Is it going to hurt you?" I asked.

"Not...as much as dying...from their venom..."

Great. Tiny *poisoned* arrows.

I pulled my knapsack over to me and took out the little pair of pliers I kept in it for when Root got himself a mouthful of porcupine quills. I hesitated for a moment, my hand hovering over a nearby twig, waiting for it to turn into a snake or who knows what. But it didn't, so I picked it up and held it near his mouth.

"Bite on this," I told him. "It'll help with the pain."

He made no response except to open his mouth. I swallowed quickly as I caught a glimpse of wicked-looking teeth. When I put the stick in his mouth, I heard the wood crunch as he bit down on it.

I moved closer and put two fingers on either side of one of the tiny arrows, grasped its shaft with the pliers, and pulled. He grunted and I heard the wood crunch again. I held the arrow up for a closer look. At least it wasn't barbed, but the tiny heads were still going to hurt as I pulled them out.

He passed out again by the time I'd gotten a dozen or so out. I felt horrible for him, but at least it let me work more quickly. I didn't have to wince in sympathy every time I pulled on one and saw the pain it caused him.

I counted the arrows as I got each one out and dropped them in a little pile on the ground by my knee. There were a hundred and thirty-seven in total.

Sitting back on my ankles, I reached forward and brushed some of the mossy hair from the little man's brow.

"What can I do now?" I asked him. "Is there someplace I can take you?"

There was no response. He was still alive—I could

tell that much by the faint rise and fall of his chest—
but that was it.

I didn't know what to do.

I assumed he had friends or family nearby, but
though I called out for a while, no one answered. I
soaked a bit of my sleeve with water from my drinking
bottle and washed his brow.

I knew I couldn't just leave him there.

"Hello! Hello!" I tried one last time.

Finally I made an envelope from a folded-up piece
of paper torn from the journal Elsie was trying to get
me to keep and carefully scooped the arrows into it,
using a twig and the little wooden trowel I'd brought
along to dig up the 'sang roots. I put it and everything else in my knapsack and slipped my arms into
the straps. Then, leaning my walking stick up against
a beech where I'd be able to easily find it when I came
back to actually harvest some 'sang, I carefully picked
up the little man and started back to Aunt Lillian's.

It was a good two hours' hike from the 'sang patch to
Aunt Lillian's. The return journey should have been

quicker because more of it was downhill, but because of the little man, it ended up taking me a lot longer. I felt I had to be careful not to jostle him too much, so I went slower than I normally would. Root would have gone mad at my pace. Every once in a while I stopped to make sure the fairy man was still breathing, then off I'd go again, wishing I was a crow and could fly straight back instead of tramping up one steep hill and down the other.

All in all, it was a disconcerting trip. I kept expecting an attack by whatever it was that had turned the little rootman into a pincushion. No matter how much I argued against it with myself, it made too much sense that his enemies would still be out here in the woods with us somewhere.

That was nerve-racking all on its own, as you can imagine, but then from time to time, the little man would suddenly become nothing more than a heap of sticks and roots and whatnot in my arms. The first time it happened I pretty near dropped him. The bundle of twigs and leaves cried out—more at my tightening grip than the sudden movement, I guess— and then he returned, the bird's nest of debris in my arms changing back into a little rootman.

"I'm sorry," I said, but he'd already drifted off on me again.

It was kind of funny, if you think about it. For three years I'd been desperate to see one of the fairy people from those stories Aunt Lillian was always telling me. But now that I had, I couldn't wait to get back to her house and be done with it. I just hoped she could figure a way out of this mess I'd found myself in, because I sensed that my troubles had just begun.

CHAPTER FOUR

t was closer to supper than lunch by the time I finally crossed the stream and started up the hill to Aunt Lillian's house.

"Oh, girl," Aunt Lillian said as I pushed the kitchen door open with my hip and came in. "What have you got us mixed up in now?"

Root lunged up from the floor but I blocked him with my leg and laid the little man down on the kitchen table.

"It's not like I did it on purpose," I said.

Aunt Lillian took charge like I'd been hoping she would. She got a swallow or two of her tonic in between his lips and rubbed his throat to make sure it went down, then wrapped the little man in a blanket and put him in a basket near the stove. Root was exiled outside the second time he came sniffing up to the basket, hoping to get him a decent look at the rootman.

"Tell me what happened," Aunt Lillian said.

We sat on either side of the basket while I explained how I'd come to be bringing the little man to her house in the first place.

"I didn't know what else to do," I said, finishing up. "I couldn't just leave him there."

Aunt Lillian had been studying the little man while I spoke. She looked up now.

"You did the right thing," she said. Her lips twitched with a smile. "Do you know what you've got here, girl?"

I shook my head.

"A 'sangman."

"You mean he's made of 'sang?"

"No. I mean he's one of the spirits we've been paying our respects to whenever we go harvesting. Looks like you finally got your wish and stepped into your own fairy story."

"I never wanted anybody to get hurt," I said.

Aunt Lillian nodded. "Guess there's always got to

be some hurt to get the story started. In my own case, I got snakebit."

I knew that one by heart, how the snake bite led to her finally meeting the Apple Tree Man and all.

"Let's have a look at those arrows," Aunt Lillian said.

I fetched the makeshift envelope from my knapsack and carefully spilled the arrows onto the top of the kitchen table. Aunt Lillian lit a lantern and brought it over. It wasn't dusk yet, but the sun was on the other side of the house, so it was dark enough to need it here. With a pair of tweezers, she picked up one of the arrows and studied it in the light.

"Lord knows I'm no expert," she said, "but I'm guessing these are bee stings."

I gave her a blank look.

"They're also called fairy shots," she explained. "These ones here are what the bee fairies use on their enemies. They don't have stingers, so they can't exactly sting the way their bees do."

"He...the 'sangman said they were poison."

Aunt Lillian nodded. "I'm sure they are. And a lot more dangerous for the likes of me or you than to another fairy."

"Do you think he's going to die?"

"I don't 'spect so. If he's still breathing after—how many of those arrows did you take out of him?"

"A hundred and thirty-seven."

"I think he'll pull through. I'm more worried about you."

I gave her a startled look. "Why me?"

"Because you've done the one thing we're never supposed to do with the fairies, girl. You've gone and stepped smack into the middle of one of their differences of opinion."

"Was I supposed to leave him to die?"

"Not according to the 'sangmen, I'd say. But the bee fairies'll have a whole other take on the situation. They're the ones we've got to worry about now."

I didn't want to think about that. I stood up.

"I've got to go," I said. "Can I leave the 'sangman with you?"

"You can't go now," Aunt Lillian said.

"But I never told Mama I was staying overnight and she'll be worried."

"Which do you 'spect would trouble her more? To have you stay here tonight—which I'm guessing she'll figure out pretty quick, even if she does feel like giving you a licking when you do get back home—or to have you dead?"

"De-dead...?"

"Think about it, girl."

"But bees don't come out at night."

"No, I don't suppose they do. But we don't know that bee fairies don't. 'Sides, I need you here for when we talk to the Apple Tree Man. We need advice from someone who's got himself an inside track on such things."

My eyes went big.

"We're going to talk to the Apple Tree Man?"

Aunt Lillian smiled. "Well, we're going to try."

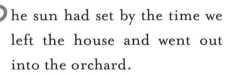

CHAPTER FIVE

*T*he sun had set by the time we left the house and went out into the orchard.

"No point us going out until after dark," Aunt Lillian had said earlier. "Folks like the Apple Tree Man aren't particularly partial to us seeing them in the daylight, don't ask me why. So we might as well have us a bite to eat."

There was a half-moon coming up over the hill behind the house as we walked through the apple trees to the oldest one in the orchard. According to Aunt Lillian, this was the Apple Tree Man's home. Unlike the other trees, she never trimmed this one. It grew in a rough tangle of gnarly limbs, surrounded by a thornbush that was half the height of the tree. I'd wondered about it choking the Apple Tree Man's tree but Aunt Lillian assured me that while we might not be able to tell the difference, he kept its growth in check.

I always like being out at night. There's a quality to moon- and starlight that makes the commonplace bigger than life, like you're seeing everything for the first time, never mind how often you've seen it before. It was no different tonight, except for the added excitement of finally having me a look at this mysterious Apple Tree Man.

We'd brought a blanket with us and I spread it on the ground while Aunt Lillian had a one-sided conversation with the tree. Anybody watching us would have thought she was just as crazy as some folks already figured she was. I guess I might have had my own questions concerning the matter if I hadn't found that little man in the 'sang patch earlier in the day.

After a while Aunt Lillian sat down on the blanket beside me, slowly easing herself down.

"I guess he's not coming," I said when we'd been sitting there a time. I didn't know if I was disappointed or relieved.

"Maybe, maybe not," Aunt Lillian said. "It's been

a while since we spoke. Could be he's just mulling over what I told him."

I wanted to ask if he really lived in the tree, if she'd really ever talked to him, but I'd always taken her stories the way she told them to me—matter-of-fact and true—and didn't want to start in on questioning her now. 'Sides, it wasn't like I could pretend this kind of thing might not be real. Not after my own adventure.

"What are you going to do when you can't stay here by yourself anymore?" I asked when we'd been sitting there awhile longer. "Where will you go?"

I was thinking of the coming winter. Looking back, I realized I'd been doing more and more work around the homestead this past summer. Not just the heavy work, but easy tasks as well. What was Aunt Lillian going to do now that I had to go back to school during the week and couldn't come out here as often?

"I 'spect I'll go live with the Apple Tree Man— unless he's moved away. Is that what's happened?" she asked in a louder voice, directed at the tree. "Did you move away? Or do you just not have the time for an old friend anymore?"

"There's no quit in you, is there, Lily Kindred?"

a strange, raspy voice suddenly asked, and I pretty near
jumped out of my skin.

Aunt Lillian's teeth flashed in the moonlight.

"Just doing my neighborly duty," she said. "Sharing news and all."

He came out from the far side of the tree and if
it hadn't been for the 'sangman I'd found, I'd have
said he was the strangest man I'd ever seen. He was as

gnarled and twisty as the limbs of his tree, long and lanky, a raggedy man with tattered clothes, bird's nest hair, and a stooped walk. It was hard to make out his features in the moonlight, but I got the sense that there wasn't a mean bone in his body—don't ask me why. I guess he just radiated a kind of goodness and charm. He acted like it was a chore, having to come out and talk to us, but I could tell he liked Aunt Lillian. Maybe missed her as much as she surely did him.

He sat down near the edge of the blanket and looked back and forth between us, his gaze finally holding on Aunt Lillian.

"So is it true?" he asked. "You've found a 'sangman?"

"I wouldn't trouble you if it wasn't true. I know how you feel about your kind and mine mixing with each other."

He looked at me. "I don't know what she might have told you, miss, but—"

"My name's Sarah Jane," I told him. "Sarah Jane Dillard."

He sighed. "But the first thing should have been not to share your name with any stranger you might happen to meet in the woods."

"He's right about that," Aunt Lillian said.

"I've heard so much about you," I said. "I didn't think you were a stranger."

"No, he's a stranger, all right," Aunt Lillian corrected me. "That's what you call folks you never see."

"The point Lily and I keep circling around like two old dogs," he said, "is that it's dangerous for humans to be with fairies. It wakes things in you that can't be satisfied, leaving you with a hunger that lasts until the end of your days, a hunger for things you can't have, or be, that only grows stronger as the years pass. It wasn't always so, but our worlds have drifted apart since the long ago when magic was simply something that filled the air instead of what it's become now: a thing that's secret and rare."

"How he goes on," Aunt Lillian said.

There was no real anger in her voice. I couldn't recall a time when she'd ever seemed really angry about anything. But I knew this old argument that lay between the two of them was something that vexed her.

The Apple Tree Man ignored her.

"How do you feel, Sarah Jane?" he asked me.

I thought it an odd sort of question until I started to consider it. How did I feel? Strange, for sure. It's disconcerting, to say the least, to find out that things you really only half believed in are real. It starts this whole domino effect in your head where you end up questioning everything. If men can step out of trees, how do I know they won't come popping out of my salad bowl when I sit down to eat? I glanced up at the moon. For all I knew, it really was made of cheese with some round-faced old fellow living in the hollowed-out center.

Who was to say where the real world stopped and fairy tales began? Maybe anything was possible.

Just thinking that made the world feel too big, the smallest thing too complicated. The ground under the blanket seemed spongy, like we could slip right into the dirt, or maybe sideways, to some fairy place, and we'd never return.

"I guess I feel different," I managed to say. "But I can't explain exactly how. It's like everything's changed and nothing has. Like I'm seeing two things at the same time, one on top of the other."

He nodded, but before he could say anything, Aunt Lillian spoke up.

"What do we do with the 'sangman?" she asked.

The Apple Tree Man turned in her direction.

"The night's full of listening ears," the Apple Tree Man said. "Perhaps we could take this indoors."

Aunt Lillian shrugged.

"You've always been welcome in my house," she said.

CHAPTER SIX

*I*f it was odd just seeing the Apple Tree Man and knowing he existed, it was odder still to have him in Aunt Lillian's house. Inside, he seemed taller than he had in the orchard. Taller, thinner. And wilder. His bird's nest hair looked twice the size it had been, with leaves and twigs and burrs and who knew what all caught up in it. He brought with him a strange feral scent. Mostly it was of apples, but underneath was a strong musk that made me feel twitchy. His knees were too tall to go under the kitchen table we all sat around, so he had to sit to the side, those long, twisty legs stretching out along the floor.

I went and got the 'sangman and set him and his

basket on the table in front of the Apple Tree Man. The little man was still unconscious, but Aunt Lillian said he seemed to be sleeping now. The Apple Tree Man agreed with her.

"They're tough little fellows, no question," he said. "Have to be to survive—how many stings was it?"

I was about to answer when we heard a low, mournful howl from outside. That was Root, I thought. He really didn't appreciate being locked up in the barn with nothing but Aunt Lillian's cow, Henny, and a handful of half-wild cats for company.

"A hundred and thirty-seven," I said.

The Apple Tree Man nodded. "So I'm thinking he must have really ticked somebody off. Usually it's no more than a sting or two, just as a reminder that they're not friends, not no way, not no how."

"Why are they feuding?" I asked.

"It's like in the song."

"Aunt Lillian said there was a song but she couldn't remember it."

"A 'sangman fell for one of the bee fairies and took her away from her hive. Everybody used to know the chorus."

He began to sing softly:

Once he took her in his arms
and kissed her long and true,
Once he took her in his arms
wasn't nothing nobody could do....

Halfway through Aunt Lillian began to sing with him. I liked the way their voices blended. It was a natural sound, like when Laurel and Bess sing together.

"That does sound a lot like 'Shady Grove,'" I said.

The Apple Tree Man smiled. "The old tunes go around and around," he said. "You can't give any of them just the one name, or the one set of words."

"So why did 'sang and bee fairies get mad at each other?" I asked. "Falling in love's supposed to be a happy thing."

The Apple Tree Man glanced at Aunt Lillian, then looked back at me.

"The bee fairy that the 'sangman in the song stole away was a princess," he said, "and the bee folk didn't much cotton to one of their highborn ladies living in the dark woods, in a hole in the ground. They've been fighting about it ever since."

"Sounds like pretty much any feud in these hills," I said. "It starts with something small and then goes on until hardly anybody remembers the whyfor. They just know they don't like each other."

The Apple Tree Man nodded. "I suppose we're not so different from you in a lot of ways."

"You can certainly be as stubborn," Aunt Lillian said.

He gave her this look again, kind of sad, kind of moony, and it got me to wondering about the two of them. Aunt Lillian never made out like there was much of anything between them 'cept friendship, but they sounded a bit like the way it could get when Adie'd run into one of her old boyfriends.

If they'd ever been a couple, I guess he'd been the one to end it. I already knew that Aunt Lillian wasn't too happy about it, but now I got the sense that maybe he wasn't, either.

"Can you take him with you?" Aunt Lillian was asking. "Let him finish his mending in your tree?"

"It's not him I'm worried about. It's you and Sarah Jane."

"Because of the bee fairies?"

The Apple Tree Man nodded. "There's no telling

what they might do when they find out you've helped him. And they will find out. Not much goes on in the meadows or the woods that they don't know about."

I didn't like to hear that. I'd always found it a little creepy in Sunday school when we were told that God was always watching us. Then I decided I didn't believe in God—or at least not the way they talked about him—and I felt like I'd gotten my privacy back. Now I had fairies to think about.

"What can we do?" Aunt Lillian asked.

"We need to find you a safe place to stay for the next couple of days—just until we can see how the land lies. We need to find a way to tell both the 'sangmen and the bee fairies that you weren't taking sides. You were just being neighborly, helping someone in their need."

"It's the truth," Aunt Lillian said.

The Apple Tree Man nodded. "But you know as well as I that sometimes the truth isn't enough."

I liked the sound of this even less.

"I can't just be going off without telling Mama where I'll be," I told them. "She's going to be mad enough I didn't come home tonight."

"I don't know what else to do," the Apple Tree

Man said. "It's too dangerous for either of you to go anywhere right now and I doubt your mama would listen to the likes of me."

Just saying she believed her eyes in the first place, I thought.

The Apple Tree Man stood and picked up the basket with the 'sangman in it.

"Come with me," he said. "And don't bother bringing anything. You'll find whatever you need where we're going."

Aunt Lillian and I exchanged glances. When she finally shrugged and stood up, I joined her. I know the Apple Tree Man said I needn't bring anything with me, but I grabbed my knapsack by its strap and brought it along all the same.

We walked back through the garden, out into the orchard. The moon was all the way on the other side of the sky now, but still shining bright enough to light our way. I couldn't tell what Aunt Lillian was feeling, but I admit I was somewhat scared my own self. Right about then, she took my hand and I felt a lot better.

I gave the thornbush a dubious look when we reached the Apple Tree Man's tree.

"Just walk through with me," he said.

All Aunt Lillian and I could do was stare at him, the way you do when someone says something that doesn't particularly make sense.

"Don't worry," he added. "What you see as barriers are only there if you think they are. It might help to shut your eyes."

I couldn't decide which would be worse, seeing where I was going or not, but in the end I did close my eyes. I counted the steps and right about where I'd reckoned the bush would be I felt something feathery tickle every inch of my skin. I guess I could have been concerned about any number of things right then, from the danger we were in to what Mama was going to say when and if I ever got myself home, but the last thing I thought about as we passed out of this world and into some other was that we'd left Root in the barn. Who was going to look after him and Henny? Who was going to feed Aunt Lillian's chickens?

And then that got swallowed up by an even bigger question, one I hadn't even considered until now, when it was too late. I started thinking in on too many of Aunt Lillian's stories and the fear rose sharp and jittery inside me. How much time was going to pass in the world outside while we were hidden away in fairyland? I didn't want to spend a day or two here and come back to find Mama and my sisters twenty years older, or worse, all long dead and gone, like that artist Aunt Lillian had met once who'd spent a couple of days in fairyland only to find twenty years had passed back here in the world he'd left behind.

But it was too late for that now.

We'd already stepped outside the world, Aunt Lillian and me both, following a smooth-talking Apple Tree Man into his tree.

opened my eyes to a buttery yellow light that seemed too bright after the dark night we'd left behind. I'd figured we'd end up right inside the tree and hadn't quite worked my mind around what it would be like, but instead of anything I might have imagined, we looked to be in somebody's house—a house that was a whole lot bigger than anything that could fit inside the trunk of any apple tree I'd ever seen. Back in the world we'd left behind, I could easily wrap my arms around its trunk, if I could get past the thorn tree protecting it. But here...here...

I was still holding hands with Aunt Lillian and we had us a look at each other, neither of us quite ready to believe what we were seeing, though there it was all the same, right in front of our noses.

"Welcome to my home," the Apple Tree Man said as he set the 'sangman's basket down by a stone hearth.

There wasn't any fire burning in it, but the big room we were in was cozy warm all the same. I looked around, trying to see where the light was coming from, but couldn't tell. It smelled like the Apple Tree Man in here, of apples and wood, with that faint underlying shiver of musk.

I guess we were in the living area of his house. The floor was polished wood with a thick hooked rug in the center. There was a pair of battered armchairs in front of the hearth with a table between them. One wall was floor-to-ceiling books, like in a library, big, fat books, all bound in leather. Later I found out they were the annals of these here hills, written by the Apple Tree Man himself, some of them.

There were a couple of paintings and a handful of framed drawings on the other walls—familiar land-scapes, I realized, as I recognized some of the sub-jects. Aunt Lillian got a funny look on her face when she spied them. She let go of my hand and walked over to give the nearest one a closer study.

Across from the hearth was a kitchen area that had a long wooden table running most of the length of the wall and all sorts of herbs and such hanging down from the rafters above it. Shelves held jars with dried mushrooms and tomatoes and I didn't know what all. There was a smaller wooden kitchen table set out a little from the longer one with a couple of ringback chairs around it. Over against another wall was a chest with clothes hooks above it. A coat as raggedy as the clothes the Apple Tree Man wore was tossed on top of the chest.

I saw two doors, but they were both closed, so I couldn't tell where they led.

"Where does the light come from?" I asked.

"Making light is one of the first things we learn," the Apple Tree Man said.

"And these paintings and drawings?" Aunt Lillian asked.

"They were gifts from a friend."

"Did you ever thank her for them?"

"I thought I did."

Aunt Lillian just made a kind of harrumphing sound. I looked back and forth between them, sensing that undercurrent of old history again. I decided it was none of my business.

"When we get back," I asked, "how much time's going to have passed?"

For a long moment, nobody answered. Those two old folks, Aunt Lillian and the Apple Tree Man, just kept on looking at each other, a conversation happening in their eyes that only they could hear. The Apple Tree Man finally shifted his gaze to me.

"The same as passes here," he said. "Time runs at different speeds throughout the Otherworld, but in this place you'll notice no difference."

That was a relief.

"What about Root?" I went on. "We left him in the barn. And Henny's going to need her milking."

"We'll worry about that in the morning. For now, have a seat by the hearth. I'll make us some tea."

"Aunt Lillian?" I said.

Maybe *he* was calm as all get-out, but I had a hundred worries and questions running through my head, and sitting around drinking tea and not talking about any of them wasn't going to help at all, so far as I could see.

"Not much else we can do right now," she said, moving away from the picture she'd been studying to take a seat in one of the two armchairs. "Might as well make ourselves comfortable."

I sighed and started to walk over to where she was sitting when a weird buzzing sound filled the air. I thought it was something of the Apple Tree Man's doing, but when I looked at him, he appeared as confused as Aunt Lillian and me. The buzzing grew louder, turning into a deep rumbling drone. We all looked around, searching for its source.

"It's the 'sangman," Aunt Lillian said.

I glanced in his direction. The little man was still lying in his basket, his mouth open. I remember thinking, Is this what a 'sangman's snores sound like? And then they came streaming out of his mouth, a yellow-and-black cloud of bees, thick as smoke, pouring out from between his lips like steam from a kettle.

"Down!" the Apple Tree Man cried. "Get down and lie still."

I knew what he meant. Elsie had told me about this before, how if you lay still on the ground, didn't so much as blink, bees that had been disturbed might just ignore you. So I did as the Apple Tree Man said and dropped to the floor. Aunt Lillian was already lying down—I never even saw her move, she must have done it so fast. The Apple Tree Man opened one of the two doors I'd seen earlier, then stretched out on the floor himself.

I tried not to even breathe as the buzzing cloud of bees circled the room at about the height of my head, had I still been standing. They made a circuit of the room, once, twice, a third time, then finally they went streaming out the door.

Long after they were gone and the Apple Tree Man had already stood up, I lay there on the floor shivering, my heart beating way too fast.

"What in tarnation was that?" Aunt Lillian said.

I sat up then and gave the 'sangman a wary glance, waiting for more of the bees to come buzzing out of his mouth, but it looked like the stream of bugs was done coming out of him. The Apple Tree Man stood up and closed the door he'd opened earlier, but not before I caught a glimpse of what lay beyond.

There was a hillside meadow out there, not much different from the one that lay outside the apple tree in Aunt Lillian's orchard, 'cept everything about it was…I don't know how to put it. More, I guess. It was like the difference between a black-and-white movie and one you see in color. That hillside pulled at me like an ache in my heart. I didn't have me but the one peek at it, but I felt myself drawn to it like no piece of land had drawn me before. I was actually on my feet and making for the door when the Apple Tree Man closed it shut.

"You don't want to go out there," the Apple Tree Man said, though we both knew that's *all* I wanted to do.

"I'd almost forgotten the ache that place can wake in a body," Aunt Lillian said.

She was looking at that closed door like her best friend had just walked out, never to return.

The Apple Tree Man shook his head. I thought it was because of what Aunt Lillian said, because of what he knew I wanted to do, but it turned out I was wrong.

"This is never going to work," he said.

"What's not?"

He looked at me. "I was going to take the two of you with me to the 'sangmen's hold. To bring the little rootman back to his kin and see if maybe they've got an idea or two that might get you out from the middle of this feud of theirs. But I can't bring you into that world. You'll never want to return. And when I do bring you back, you'll spend the rest of your lives heartsick for the wanting of it."

I didn't argue. That one glimpse I got made me think what he was saying might well be true. But Aunt Lillian was buying none of it.

"You need to give us a little more credit than that," she said. "Sure, we've got the wanting to be in that place. And maybe, when we come back, we'll even be pining for it. But we're stronger than you think. Everybody lives without things they figure they're desperate to have. That's just part of living. The sick person wants to be well. The rejected suitor can't stop thinking of the girl who turned him down. One person needs a fat bank account, another what that money might buy.

"We don't get what we want, life still goes on. We make do. We don't shut down and lie in a corner and cry for the rest of our lives."

"Some do," the Apple Tree Man said. "Some people come back and they're never happy again."

"Maybe," Aunt Lillian replied. "But I'm not one of them. And I find it insulting how you keep on insisting I am—like somehow you know me better than I know my own self."

"I just think—"

"Too much sometimes," Aunt Lillian said. "No

reason to be ashamed of it. It's a failing common to my people as well."

They stood there looking at each other, no give in either of them, until finally the Apple Tree Man gave a slow nod.

"My apologies," he said. "I should learn to take folks at their word."

"Would surely simplify a lot of things," Aunt Lillian agreed.

"And you?" the Apple Tree Man asked, turning to me.

I looked at Aunt Lillian, but she shook her head.

"I can't help you here, girl," she said. "This is one of those things that each of us needs to work out on our own. You understand what I mean?"

I nodded. I didn't like it, but I knew what she meant. I turned my attention to the Apple Tree Man.

"I guess the bees will be out there," I said.

"But they won't be concerned with us," he said. "Not unless we run into the bee fairies before we reach the 'sangmen's hold."

"How did they get to be inside the 'sangman in the first place?" I asked.

"It's part of the bee-sting magic. Their fairy shots

are poison, through and through—there's no deny-
ing that. But they also give rise to new tribes of bees.
What we saw coming out of the 'sangman was like a
new hive—born in fairy blood and bee venom and
now out swarming to make themselves a new home.
They're going to be too busy to bother with the likes
of us unless someone sets them on us."

"That's not where bees come from," I said.

I was always a good listener and I could remember
any number of Elsie's stories about bees, from the
old bee gum hives that people once made with the
hollowed sections of black gum tree trunks, to how
the best honey came from the nectar of sourwood
tree blossoms.

"It's where those came from," the Apple Tree
Man said. "If you hadn't pulled out all those arrows,
they would have consumed the 'sangman before they
swarmed. As it is, there was just enough venom in him
to make a small swarm, but not enough to harm him."

"But—"

"You're stalling," Aunt Lillian said.

I was. The truth was, I didn't know if I could do
it. I didn't know if I was as strong as Aunt Lillian.
I found myself remembering one of those stories

of hers, the one about folks crossing over, how they came back either poets or crazy, and I sure couldn't rhyme more than the odd verse or two of doggerel.

"You can wait for us here," the Apple Tree Man said.

I thought Aunt Lillian would take offense to that, considering how she'd been going on earlier about us being stronger than the Apple Tree Man gave us credit for. But she just gave me a kind look.

"There's no shame in staying behind," she said. "Considering all the stories about the trouble one can get into on the other side, maybe it makes more sense to stay clear of that land."

I could tell she meant it. That she wasn't going to think less of me if I stayed behind. But that stubborn Dillard streak wouldn't let me off the hook as easily as Aunt Lillian would.

"No," I said, wondering if I'd live to regret it. "I've got to see this through now."

Nobody asked if I was sure or tried to argue me out of it. Aunt Lillian just gave me an encouraging smile. The Apple Tree Man picked up the 'sangman's basket and off we went, through the door and away.

Awful Sharp Thing,
a Bee Is

CHAPTER EIGHT

Adie and Elsie

I'm starting to get worried," Mama said.

Adie shrugged, a gesture that was lost on her mother since Adie was lying on the couch, idly flipping through a magazine while watching some boy band on the music-video channel with Laurel and Bess.

"Oh, you know Janey," she said. "She'll jump at any chance she can get to be up at that old woman's place."

"She didn't say she was staying overnight. I'm going to have words with that girl when you bring her back."

Adie sat up straight. "When *I* bring her back? Why do I have to go? Elsie's our nature girl. She loves chances to go into the woods."

"I'm sure she does. And you can certainly take Elsie or any of the other girls with you. But you're the oldest and if something happened to Sarah Jane on the way back from Lily's place, I'd feel better knowing you were there to deal with the problem."

Adie had to smile. That was Mama for you. Always making you feel like something you didn't much care to do was actually something special that only you could do for her. Even knowing this trick of Mama's, Adie couldn't quell the flicker of pride that rose up in her.

Closing her magazine, she got up to find her running shoes.

"And take this with you," Mama said when Adie had her shoes and coat on and was making for the door. "You can put it in a knapsack."

Adie sighed when she saw the jar of preserves and bag of muffins Mama was holding out to her. It seemed like you couldn't say hello to someone on the road around here without exchanging some kind of food or other. But she dutifully fetched a knapsack and loaded it up.

"And no dawdling," Mama said. "You tell Sarah Jane she's to come straight home."

Adie rolled her eyes. "There's nothing to dawdle over between here and Aunt Lillian's."

"Be that as it may..."

"See, this is why we need a cell phone. If we had one right now, we could just call Janey and tell her to get her butt back home."

Mama smiled. "And you'd be happy with her taking it with her whenever she goes to see Lily?"

Adie thought about how often her sister went to the old woman's place and shook her head.

"I'll just go get her," she said.

⌒

She found Elsie in the pasture, carefully drawing a study of some little animal's skull she'd discovered in the grass. Mouse, vole—Adie couldn't tell. Elsie was still like a kid about this. She'd just get all excited about finding a nest or a feather or some animal's skeleton. But she knew more about what went on in the fields and woods around the farm than any of them. Adie supposed there was something to say about paying the kind of attention Elsie did to every little thing she came across in her wanderings.

"Come on, skinny knees," she said. "Mama says we've got to go look for Janey."

"Just a sec."

She waited while Elsie finished her drawing, made a notation under it, and dated it, then carefully stowed away her pencil and journal in her own knapsack.

"How come we have to get her?" Elsie asked.

She stood up, brushing grass and dirt from the knees of her jeans.

"She never came home last night and Mama's worried."

"I just thought she was staying over."

"Well, she forgot to tell Mama that, so we're stuck fetching her back."

"You don't think anything's happened to her, do you?"

Adie thought of teasing her, but then realized that she felt a little nag of worry herself.

"What could happen to her between here and there?" she asked.

She held up her hand as Elsie was about to answer. Elsie, being the family expert on everything that grew or lived in these hills, could probably come up with a hundred things that might have gone wrong.

"No," she said quickly. "I don't need to know. Everything's going to be fine. We'll find her and

Aunt Lillian hoeing the garden or shucking peas or whatever it is that they do up at that place to keep themselves busy."

⌒

But they didn't.

It was strangely quiet around the Kindred homestead an hour or so later, when they came into the last meadow and started up the hill to the house. The little nagging feeling in Adie's chest blossomed into real worry as they called out ahead and got no answer. It grew stronger still when they heard Root barking from the barn. There was a frantic quality to his voice that made Adie's pulse beat way too fast.

The two girls ran to the barn, fumbling to unbar the door. When they finally got the bar off and the door open, Root bounded by them and took off up the hill, running into the orchard. Adie and Elsie exchanged worried glances, then hurried after him. They found him whining by an old apple tree half choked with thornbushes, lying with his head on his paws as he stared at the tree.

"What is it, boy?" Adie asked. "What's wrong?"

"That's the Apple Tree Man," Elsie said.

"The what?"

"The Apple Tree Man. It's what Aunt Lillian calls the oldest tree in the orchard."

"And that means?"

Elsie shrugged. "I don't know. It's just what she calls it."

Adie looked away from the tree, back to the house. She didn't come up here very often. It wasn't that she disliked Aunt Lillian. She just found it too weird up here. You couldn't even use the bathroom to have a pee, because there wasn't one. There was only the outhouse, where you *knew* there was a spider getting ready to climb onto your butt as soon as you sat down. Adie couldn't imagine living without electricity or running water—especially not on purpose.

"It's too quiet," she said.

"It's always quiet up here," Elsie said, but she sounded doubtful.

Adie knew just what she was thinking. There was something wrong, but neither of them wanted to say it aloud.

"I guess we should check the house," she said.

Elsie nodded.

Adie remembered what Mama'd said to get her to come up here.

You're the oldest and if something happened to Sarah Jane on the way back from Lily's place, I'd feel better knowing you were there to deal with the problem.

Maybe she was the oldest, but she didn't know where to start right now. She didn't feel at all capable. All she felt was panic.

She swallowed hard.

"They're just inside, where they can't hear us," she said.

"Then why did they lock Root up in the barn?"

"I don't know, okay?"

Elsie looked like she was about to burst into tears.

"I'm sorry," Adie said quickly. "I'm worried, too."

She took her sister's hand and started off toward the house.

"Come on, Root," she called over her shoulder.

But the dog wouldn't budge. All he did was stare at that stupid old tree and whine.

"Everything's going to be fine," she assured Elsie as they approached the house. "They're probably just gone off hunting berries or something."

Elsie nodded. "That's right. Janey said they were

going out after 'sang yesterday. Maybe they went today instead."

"There. You see? There's nothing for us to worry about."

They both jumped at a sudden loud, moaning sound, then laughed when they saw it was just Aunt Lillian's cow having followed them up from the barn. Henny lowed again, long and mournfully.

"She sounds like she wants something," Adie said.

"Maybe she needs to be milked."

"But they would have done that before they left." Elsie nodded.

They were on the porch now.

"Hello!" Adie called inside. "Is anybody home?"

They went inside, nervous again. They found no one on the ground floor, and neither of them wanted to check the upstairs.

"This looks like last night's dinner dishes," Elsie said as they looked around the kitchen.

Adie dropped her knapsack by the door and nodded. "I guess we need to look upstairs."

Reluctantly, they went up the stairs, wincing at every creak the old wood made under their feet. The stairs took them into an open loft of a room. This had been where Aunt Lillian slept until her own aunt Em passed away. Now it was just used for storage, though there was little enough of it. Some old books. Winter clothes hanging on a pole and draped in plastic. By the window there was a large trunk.

"There," Adie said, only barely keeping the relief out of her voice. "You see? There's no one here."

"What about the trunk?"

"You think someone's hiding in the trunk?"

Elsie shook her head. "But you could put a...you know..."

She didn't need to say the word. It sprang readily to Adie's mind. Yes, the trunk was big enough to hold a body.

Crossing the floor, Adie went over to it, hesitated only a moment, then flung it open.

"Still nothing," she said. "And nobody, either. There's just a mess of drawings."

Elsie joined her by the open trunk and looked inside. She picked up the top drawings.

"These are really good. Who do you think did them?"

Adie shrugged. "Who knows? Maybe Aunt Lillian."

"I didn't know she could draw."

Elsie continued to explore the trunk while Adie used the vantage of a second-floor window to see if she could spy any sign of Aunt Lillian or their missing sister.

Under the loose drawings Elsie found numerous sketchbooks, each page filled with sketches of the hills around the house. They were like what Elsie did in her own journal, cataloging the flora and fauna, only the drawings were so much better than hers. Further in, she found stacks of oil paintings on wood panels—color studies done in the field in preparation for work that would be realized more fully in a studio. Under them were still more drawings and sketchbooks. Many of these had a childlike quality to them and were done on scraps of brown paper and cardboard.

She looked at the paintings again. There was something familiar about them. When she came to one depicting a black bear in a meadow clearing, she caught a sharp breath.

"What is it?" Adie asked.

"I've seen the finished painting this was done for. Or at least I've seen a picture of it in a magazine. The original's hanging in the Newford Museum of Art. But that means…"

She started looking more carefully through the paintings and drawings and began to recognize more of the sketches as studies for paintings she'd seen in various books and magazines. Finally she found what she was looking for inside one of the earlier sketchbooks.

"Look at this," she said.

Adie gave the pages a quick study. From what she could tell, somebody had been doodling various ways to write their initials.

"L.M.," she read. "What does that stand for do you think?"

"Lily McGlure."

"And she is?"

"Apparently the name that Aunt Lillian painted under," Elsie said.

"I thought she was a Kindred."

"I don't know about that. Maybe she changed her name. Maybe it's just a pen name. But this is amazing."

"Why?"

"*Why?*" Elsie repeated. "The Aunt Lillian we know is really Lily McGlure. What could be more amazing than that?"

"So?"

"So she's famous. They often talk about her like she was one of the Newford Naturalists, even though her work was done a few decades after their heyday. But you can see why, when you look at her paintings."

Adie couldn't, really, but she didn't want to seem more ignorant than she probably already did, so she said nothing.

"She's supposed to have studied with both Milo Johnson and Frank Spain," Elsie went on, "though there's some dispute about that, considering how they disappeared at least twenty years before she started to paint seriously."

"How do you know all this stuff?"

"I don't know," Elsie said. "I like to read about art and watch the Discovery Channel. I just find it interesting, I guess."

Adie gave the trunk a thoughtful look.

"When you said these two artists disappeared," she said, "what did you mean?"

"Oh, it's one of the big mysteries of the Newford art world. They were out painting in the hills around here and they just vanished...." Elsie's voice trailed off and she gave her sister an anguished look.

"We don't know that anything happened to Janey or Aunt Lillian," Adie said. "I'm sure it's just like we thought, they're out hunting 'sang." She took the sketchbook from Elsie's hands and put it back in the trunk. "Come on. Let's close this up and go back outside."

Elsie nodded. She placed the drawings and paintings back on top of the sketchbooks. Closing the trunk lid, she stood up and followed Adie back to the stairs.

"What do we do now?" she asked. "Do we stay? Do we go looking for them? Do we go home?"

"See, this is why we really need a cell phone," Adie said. "Or even two. We could call Mama right now and ask her what to do."

"But we can't."

"I know. Let me think a minute."

They stood out on the porch, looking out across the garden to the orchard, where Root still kept his vigil by the old apple tree.

"We should put the cow back in the barn," Elsie said. "Or at least in the pasture."

Right now the cow was in the garden, munching on the runner beans that grew up a pair of home-made cedar trellises on the far side of the corn.

Adie nodded and fell in step beside her sister. "There sure seem to be a lot of bees around here to-day," she said as they reached the garden.

Elsie grabbed the cow's halter and drew her away from the beans.

"They're gathering the last of the nectar," she explained, "so that they'll have enough honey to get them through the winter."

"I suppose," Adie said. "But these don't seem to be collecting much nectar. It looks to me like they're just flying around."

Elsie studied the bees. Adie was right. The bees were ignoring the last of the asters and such and seemed...well, they seemed to be searching for some-thing, but for what, Elsie couldn't tell.

"That's just weird," she said.

"Everything about this morning is weird," Adie said. "From the way Root's acting and these bees, to how there's just nobody around."

Elsie nodded. "I think we should put Henny back into the barn and go home. Mama will know what to do."

"I suppose."

Adie hated the idea of having to turn to their mother for help. She liked the idea that Mama was there if they should need her, but she much preferred to solve her problems on her own.

They were halfway back to the barn when Adie suddenly put her hand on Elsie's arm.

"Do you hear that?" she asked.

She needn't have bothered. Elsie had already stopped and turned to look at the woods beyond the orchard herself.

"It sounds like bells," she said.

Adie nodded. Bells and the jingle of bridles. And now that they and the cow had stopped moving, they could also hear the faint hollow sound of hooves on the ground. Many hooves. Adie reached for Elsie's hand, to take comfort as well as give it, when the riders came into view.

They were like knights and great ladies out of some medieval storybook. The men weren't wearing armor, but they still had the look of knights in their yellow-

and-black livery, with their plumed helmets and silvery shields. The women didn't ride sidesaddle, but they wore long, flowing dresses that streamed down the flanks of their horses and trailed on the ground behind them. On either side of the riders ranged long-legged, golden-haired dogs with black markings—some cross between greyhounds and wolves.

Neither the riders nor their animals seemed quite right. They were all too tall, too lean, their features too sharp. A nimbus of shining golden light hung about them, unearthly and bright. The whole company—men and women, their mounts and all—were so handsome it was hard to look at them and not feel diminished. Adie and Elsie felt like poor country cousins invited to a palatial ballroom, standing awkwardly in the doorway, not wanting to come in.

"This can't be real," Adie said.

Elsie made no reply except to squeeze her hand.

The riders came down from the meadow, footmen running along behind, and encircled the two girls. The footmen notched arrows in their bows, aiming at Adie and Elsie.

"Well, that was easy enough," said the woman who appeared to be leading them.

CHAPTER NINE

Laurel and Bess

t never made much sense to Laurel that they would still be weeding the garden in September when most of the vegetables had already been harvested. But that was the chore Mama had set her and Bess while the younger twins were in charge of cleaning the house.

Of course they weren't just weeding. They were also gathering errant potatoes and turnips and the like that had been missed during the earlier harvest, putting them in a basket to take inside later. When they were done weeding, they were supposed to turn the soil on the sections they'd weeded. After that, one or more of the other girls would spread compost over it all and that would be it until spring. Mama liked a tidy garden, everything neat and ready for next year's planting.

"We should've gone with Adie and Elsie," Laurel said.

Bess shrugged. "This'd still be waiting for us when we got back."

"I know. But I'm bored. This whole weekend's just all too boring."

Last night's dance at the Corners had been canceled, no one was exactly sure why. But there were rumors and gossip, as always. Bess had heard from the postman that the building had become infested with rats and so the county had closed it down. Martin Spry, a fiddler who lived down the road from them, had told Laurel that someone had vandalized the place the night before and the police were still investigating. But Mama said all of that was nonsense.

"Mrs. Timmons told me the Jacksons got called out of town," she said. "Something about one of their grandkids getting sick, and by the time they heard, it was too late to get anyone to take over for the night. That's all."

Maybe, maybe not, Laurel thought. All she knew was that they hadn't gotten to play out since last weekend. Hadn't been playing, hadn't been dancing. All they had to look forward to were school starting, chores, and watching interchangeable videos on the music channel.

Laurel leaned on her hoe. "I really wanted to play that medley of Ziggy Stardust tunes that we worked out—just to see the faces on the old fiddlers."

The twins loved the old tunes and songs, but they also had an inordinate fondness for music from the seventies and eighties, which they kept trying to shoehorn into old-timey arrangements with varying degrees of success—everything from Pink Floyd to punk and disco.

"Instead," Laurel said, "all we have is boredom."

"Way too much, too," Bess agreed.

"If only something interesting could happen around here."

It was at precisely that moment, as though called up like an answered wish, that they heard the fiddle music come drifting down the hill and across the pastures to where they were working in the garden. The twins lifted their heads as one.

"Do you hear that?" Laurel asked.

"I'm not deaf."

"Who do you suppose it is?"

"Don't know," Bess said. "But it's not Marty."

Laurel nodded. "The tone's too sweet to be him."

"Doesn't sound like anyone we know," Bess added after they'd listened a little more.

Not only was the player unfamiliar, but so were the tunes. And that was irresistible.

Laurel laid down her hoe. "Are you thinking what I'm thinking?"

"Always."

Bess brushed her hands on her jeans, and the two of them went into the house to collect their instruments.

CHAPTER TEN

Ruth and Grace

uth leaned on the windowsill she was supposed to be dusting and watched Laurel and Bess walk toward the woods with their instrument cases in hand.

"How come they get to blow off their chores while we're stuck in here?" she said.

Her twin, Grace, joined her at the window. "They just thought of it first, I guess."

"I guess. Hey, you know what would be funny? If we went down and put all those taters and such back in the ground."

Grace shook her head. "Too much work. You know what would be funnier?"

"What?"

"If someone hid their instruments and replaced them in their cases with stones wrapped up in T-shirts so the cases would still weigh the same."

Ruth turned to her twin with a grin. "You didn't."

"I'm not saying I did or didn't. I'm just saying it would be funny." She paused, then grinned as well. "But I sure thought they'd find out before now."

"If there'd been a dance last night," Ruth began.

Grace nodded. "And there they'd be, invited up onstage and opening their cases."

They started to giggle and slid down onto the floor with their backs to the wall, unable to stop, the one constantly setting the other off.

CHAPTER ELEVEN

Laurel and Bess

ama's going to kill us," Bess said as the sisters started across the pasture. She carried her banjo case with an easy familiarity to its weight.

"Only if she catches us," Laurel said. "I figure we've got two or three hours, maybe longer if she stops in to see Mrs. Runion."

Bess smiled. Mrs. Runion was a sweet old woman who lived on the edge of town and could talk your ear off if you gave her half the chance. Granny Burrell used to say that she'd been born talking, but Mama never seemed to mind. Mama was like Janey, in that she enjoyed visiting with old folks, saying, "All our history lives in those who've been around as long as Mrs. Runion. When we lose them, we lose a piece of our history, unless we take the time to listen to what they've got to tell us."

Bess supposed she half understood. She and Laurel felt the same about music and, while they weren't much for sitting around chatting with someone like Mrs. Runion, they saw nothing odd about making a two-mile hike up some bush road to spend the afternoon and evening listening to some old fellow scratch out tunes on his fiddle, or maybe rasp his way through one of the old ballads.

Music was something that needed to be passed along, too. Or at least the old songs and tunes did.

"She hasn't seen Mrs. Runion for a couple of weeks," Bess said, "so it's a good bet she'll stop in today."

Laurel nodded. "Will you listen to that fiddler play."

"I haven't heard a tune I know yet," Bess said.

"I just can't imagine who it would be, out in our woods like this."

Bess laughed. "Maybe it's one of Aunt Lillian's fairy people."

"You'd think Janey would have grown out of those stories by now."

"You'd think, but you'd be wrong."

They reached the woods and followed a deer trail that wound back and forth up the side of the hill. With each step they took, the fiddling grew louder, and they marveled at the player's skill. The bass strings resonated, rich and full. The notes drawn from the high strings skirled up among the turning leaves into the autumn sky. There was so much rhythm in the playing that adding a guitar or a banjo wasn't even necessary.

Grinning at each other, they hurried forward. Finally they knew they were almost upon the fiddler and they vibrated with anticipation. The trail they followed took them into a clearing, and there in the middle, where this path crossed another, stood the oddest little man.

He was maybe three feet tall and looked like a walking shrub, a bark and leafy man playing a fiddle almost half the size of himself. They couldn't tell where the wood of his instrument ended and his limbs began. He seemed to have moss and leaves for hair, gnarly twigs for fingers—but oh, how they pulled the tune from his fiddle.

He stopped playing at their sudden arrival and the three of them looked at each other for a long moment, none of them speaking, none of them moving or so much as even breathing.

This can't be right, Bess thought. She knew that such a fiddler couldn't possibly exist, but her head was too clouded and fuzzy to feel alarmed. Beside her, Laurel appeared to be just as spellbound.

It was something in the music, a faraway part of Bess's mind whispered. That, she was sure, was the source of the spell.

Belatedly, she was also aware that the spot where the two deer trails met might well be considered a crossroads, and there were any number of stories about the sorts of people you met at a crossroads. Like Old Bubba, ready to trade you the gift of music for your soul as he had with Robert Johnson. The fiddler didn't look like Old Bubba himself, but she wouldn't be surprised if a body came walking up and told her he was some kind of devil man.

Oh, danger, danger, the little voice in her head whispered, but she couldn't seem to move, never mind run away.

"So you like music?" the little man said.

As soon as he spoke, Bess found she could breathe again. She didn't trust her legs to carry her far, but at least she could breathe.

"We love music," Laurel said.

"And play it, too, by the looks of those cases."

"We play some."

"Just exactly what are you?" Bess asked.

"A fiddler, what did you think? Get out your instruments and we'll play us a tune."

"I don't know that we should," Bess said softly to her sister as they laid their cases on the ground. "There's something not right here."

Laurel shrugged. "We're just seeing that Aunt Lillian didn't make up all those stories of hers that Janey keeps telling us."

"I figure we should be feeling a little more scared than I am."

"What? Of him? He's not much bigger than a minute."

"But he'll be magic. It was magic brought us here."

Laurel shook her head. "Wasn't magic brought me—it was music."

"Same difference," Bess said.

"I tell you what," the little man said, either ignoring

their whispered conversation or not hearing it. "Why don't we make us a bargain? If the two of you can play me a tune I've never heard before, I'll grant you one wish, whatever it is you want."

"And if we can't?" Laurel asked.

"Then you come away with me," the little man told them.

"How do we know you can deliver?" Laurel asked.

"What do you lose to find out? A bright pair of girls like you must know a thousand tunes."

Bess pulled at Laurel's arm when she realized that Laurel was actually considering the little man's bet. Her sister had to be more deeply snared by his magic than she was to even think of agreeing to this.

"This is stupid," she said. "Nobody ever wins this sort of thing."

"It seems pretty straightforward to me," Laurel said.

"It is," the little man said. "But it has to be done here, and it has to be done now."

"Laurel," Bess began.

But her sister shook her head. "This is a sure thing. If we can't play him a tune he doesn't know, we deserve to be taken away." She turned to the little man.

"You're on, mister. Get that wish ready."

She unbuckled the clasps of her fiddle case, lifted the lid, then shot an angry glance at the little man. All that was in her case were stones wrapped in a few T-shirts. Her fiddle was gone.

"That's cheating," she said.

Bess quickly opened her own case to find that her banjo was gone as well, replaced by similar stones wrapped in T-shirts.

"Forfeit," the little man said. "Now you come with me."

"No," Laurel said. "You cheated. What did you do with our instruments?"

"I did nothing to them."

"Then lend me yours."

"Of course."

He handed over his fiddle but there were so many little vines and twigs and leaves growing out of it that Laurel could barely get a note out of a string by plucking it. Bowing was out of the question.

The little man snatched his instrument back and stowed it away in a bag that was lying on the ground by his feet. He put his bow in after, then tied up the sack and slung it over his shoulder.

"No more dawdling," he said. "Come along."

He held out a hand to each of them.

The twins began to back away, but he was quick and far stronger than he looked. He grabbed each by an arm.

"You're a lying cheat!" Laurel cried.

She aimed a kick at him but it hurt her toe through her running shoe more than it seemed to hurt him.

"I don't lie and I don't cheat," the little man said.

He said something else in a language neither girl could understand. They both grew dizzy, but before they could fall, the little man pulled them away, out of the world they knew and into his own. A moment later, all that remained at the crossroads were two open instrument cases filled with stones.

CHAPTER TWELVE

Ruth and Grace

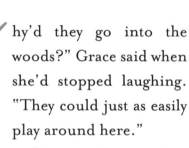

hy'd they go into the woods?" Grace said when she'd stopped laughing. "They could just as easily play around here."

"Because this way they won't have us bugging them."

"They think," Grace said.

"They dream."

"I can't wait to see their faces when they open those cases of theirs."

Ruth shot her a big grin.

Jumping to their feet, the pair ran downstairs and outside. Playing Indian scout as they followed the older twins was way more fun than cleaning house.

They hid behind clumps of milkweed and tall grasses and Joe Pye weed, darting from one to the next, trying hard not to giggle too loudly and give themselves away.

"There sure are a lot of hornets around today," Ruth said as they reached the deer trail their sisters had taken.

"Those aren't hornets, they're bees."

"What*ever*."

"But you're right," Grace agreed. "There are lots of them. There's probably a nest nearby."

"Hive."

Grace stuck out her tongue. "What*ever*."

They'd heard a fiddle play the whole time they'd been crossing the fields. Here in the woods it was louder, but it didn't do the same for them as it had for Laurel and Bess. Pure, simple curiosity pulled them along the trail.

"Looks like they're planning to have a hooley in the woods," Ruth said.

Grace nodded. "Probably with a bunch of those old coots they're always playing with."

"Martin's not an old coot. I think he's handsome."

"But he plays the fiddle."

"Lots of nice people play the fiddle."

"Name one."

"Laurel."

"She doesn't count. She's our sister."

"Well, how about—"

"Shh!"

Ruth fell silent, realizing what Grace already had: They were too close to keep nattering on the way they were.

The fiddling had stopped and they could hear voices. They crept along the path until it opened into a small meadow, and then they stood there with their mouths agape, staring at the little man with the fiddle that their older sisters had come to meet. Finally, Grace tugged on Ruth's arm, pulling her down, out of sight behind a bush. The two girls looked at each other, eyes wide.

"That...man," Ruth said in a voice that was barely a whisper. "He can't be real...can he?"

Grace shook her head.

"But there he is all the same," she said just as quietly.

"And Laurel and Bess know him. Came to meet him in the woods and all."

"I don't think they know him. Listen."

They heard Laurel make her bargain with the man. When she and Bess laid down their cases, Grace began to shiver.

"Oh no, oh no, oh no," she said, burrowing her face in Ruth's shoulder.

Ruth looked over her sister's head, understanding immediately. Playing that trick with the older twins' instruments wasn't funny anymore. It wasn't funny at all.

And then...then the little man pulled their two sisters away into thin air. They were there one moment, gone the next, as though they'd all stepped behind an invisible curtain.

Ruth pressed her cheek against Grace's, trying hard not to cry because Grace was doing enough for the both of them. She held Grace close, trying to breathe slowly like Mama said they should do when they felt upset. "People forget to breathe," she'd say, "and then they can't think straight anymore. They get mad when they should be patient. Or do something stupid when they could have been smart."

"Breathe, breathe," she said to Grace.

Slowly she could feel the panic ebb a little. She sat back and held Grace at arm's length to see that her sister was getting a hold of herself as well.

"That…that was real…wasn't it?" Grace finally said.

Ruth had to swallow before she replied. "Looks like."

"It's my fault. They could've played rings around that little man."

"You didn't know."

"It's still my fault."

"It doesn't matter anymore," Ruth said. "All that matters now is that we figure out a way to get them back."

Grace nodded. "I wish Janey was here."

"Me, too."

Janey wasn't the oldest, but she knew all the stories. She got them from Aunt Lillian and was happy to pass them along to anyone who wanted to listen, which, in the Dillard family, pretty much only meant their older sister Elsie, who liked them, and Mama, who always seemed to have the time to listen to anything any one of them had to say.

Ruth stood up. "Come on," she said. "We can at least look for clues."

"Clues? Suddenly we're detectives?"

"You know what I mean."

She walked into the meadow with Grace trailing after her. They touched the instrument cases with the toes of their shoes and walked all around the spot where the little man and their sisters had disappeared, but there was nothing to see.

"I guess we have to go home and get Mama to help," Ruth said.

Grace gave a glum nod.

They turned to the instrument cases, meaning to close them up and bring them along, when they realized that they were no longer alone.

Right where the deer trail came out of the woods stood another little man. But where the one who had kidnapped their sisters looked like a piece of a tree that decided to go for a walk, this one seemed more human. If you discounted his size. And the fact that he had virtually no neck. His round ball of a head seemed to sit directly on the round ball of his body. And then there were the wings—almost as big as him, fluttering rapidly at his back.

He looked, Ruth decided, a lot like a bee, what with the shape of his body and the wings and the fact that his shirt and trousers were all yellow and black stripes. She remembered all the bees they'd noticed on the way to this place. Were they *all* some kind of weird were-bees? She gave the meadow a quick study, but other than the fact that there seemed to be more bees than usual, the little man appeared to be on his own.

"Well, now," the little man said. "The 'sangman got your sisters, and that made us even, but now we've got you, so we're ahead again."

Grace stooped and picked up one of the stones from Laurel's fiddle case.

Ruth quickly followed suit. Oddly enough, she didn't feel scared. She just felt angry now. Breathe, she started to tell herself, but then she realized she didn't want to stop being angry.

"What?" she asked. "Are you on some kind of sick scavenger hunt?"

The bee man gave her a puzzled look.

"Because if you are—" Grace said. "If you think you're taking us anywhere, we'll knock your brains right out of your head."

She hefted the stone she was holding to show him she meant business.

He held his hands up. "No, no. You can't do that. You're my captives."

"Not likely," Grace said.

But Ruth heard a buzzing and now Grace did, too. The bees that had been flying about the meadow earlier were all hovering nearby now. And not just a handful, but hundreds and hundreds of them.

"I don't think we have enough stones," Ruth said. "Not to hit them all."

"Probably not," Grace replied. "But we can hit him."

"You don't want to do that," the bee man said. "Please. You need to calm down. No one will hurt you if you'll just come along quietly."

"We don't want to go anywhere," Ruth said.

"But you don't have any choice."

"Where do you want to take us?" Grace asked.

"Yeah, and why?" Ruth added.

"You're hostages, nothing more."

Ruth shook her head. "You don't want to mess with us," she said. "We've got a big brother, you know, and he's killed thirteen giants."

"No, you don't," the bee man said.

"Yes, we do," Grace said. "He's tall and fierce and he eats bees like candy. Eats them by the handful."

"He eats bee sandwiches," Ruth added. "And bee soup."

"Bee stew and deep-fried bees."

"And he loves fat little bee men best of all."

"You don't have a brother," the bee man said. "Why would you pretend that you do?"

"Why are we supposed to be your hostages?" Grace asked.

"Yeah," Ruth said. "And what are we being hostaged for?"

"I don't think that's a word," Grace said.

"He knows what I mean."

"Your sister has the 'sangman prince," the bee man said, "and we need something to trade to her for him."

"So trade yourself."

"Or some of your bees," Grace added.

"And," the bee man went on, "if we didn't take you, the 'sangmen would. So you're actually safer with us."

"What are these 'sangmen?" Ruth asked. "Are they like the weird little guy who grabbed our sisters just now?"

The bee man nodded. "They're evil, rooty crea-tures."

"And you're just a bundle of sunshine and joy," Grace said.

"At least we don't take children of the light and put them in a dark hole."

"I think you're making this all up," Ruth said. "I think the two of you are in cahoots. You and this singsong man."

"'Sangman."

"Don't you start correcting me," Ruth told him. "You're not family."

"You're in danger," the bee man tried.

"Oh, right. Like we need to be protected from these singsong men."

"Whatever they think they are," Grace put in.

"When what we really need is to be protected from you and your little buzzy friends."

"I think we should bop him with a stone and take our chances," Grace said.

"They've already stolen two of you," the bee man said, "and put a glamour on your sister so that she thinks she needs to help them."

"Which sister?" Ruth asked.

"Probably Els—"

Grace was cut off by the jab of Ruth's elbow in her side.

"Remember in the war movies," Ruth said. "Name, rank, and serial number. That's all we're supposed to give the enemy."

Grace nodded and looked at the bee man.

"I'm Grace, daughter number six," she said.

Ruth shook her head. "You just love to rub in that you were born one minute earlier, don't you?"

"I'm not your enemy," the bee man said. "Please believe me."

"At least he's polite," Ruth said. "For a kidnapper and all."

"If you'll just come with me, the queen will explain everything."

"Oh, now he's got a queen," Grace said.

"Well, he is a bee man. I wonder what it's like to live in a hive."

"Very noisy, I'd say."

"That's enough!" the bee man cried. "I don't know why I had to get picked for this stupid job, but I'm finishing it now."

He made
a few odd
movements
with his hands
and the bees
swept in over
the girls, covering
their faces, necks,
and arms, leaving
open circles around
their eyes and mouths.
"Don't move!" he warned them.
"Don't even breathe or my little cousins will give you
a thousand stings, and you'll like that even less than
being captured."

Ruth stared at the bees covering her hands and
then gasped. Riding each bee was a miniature version
of the bee man who stood in front of them, each with
a bow and a notched arrow. She turned her gaze to
meet Grace's. They didn't have to speak. They each
dropped the stone they were holding.

"That's better," the bee man said. "Now follow
me."

He made another odd movement with his hands

and the air began to shimmer, just as it had when the
'sangman had stolen away the older twins.

"I think we're in real trouble now," Grace said.

Ruth wanted to nod, but she was too scared to move
in any way except for how the bee man told them to.

"We should have left a note for Mama," she said.

Then she and Grace followed the bee man into the
shimmering air, and the world they knew was gone.

CHAPTER THIRTEEN

Adie and Elsie

Deeper in the woods and higher up in the hills, there was no opportunity for Adie or Elsie to have any sort of discussion with their captors.

Their queen had neither the interest nor the patience for dialogue with her captives. As soon as Adie started to ask a question, the queen waved a long, thin hand in her direction.

"Gag her," she said. "Gag them both and bind their wrists."

Footmen with ropes and strips of cloth ran from behind the horses to carry out her orders. Adie called out to the queen before they reached her and Elsie.

"Please," she said. "We'll be quiet. Don't gag us."

The queen studied her for a long moment, then gave a brisk nod.

"No gags," she told the footmen. "But bind their wrists and if they speak out of turn again, gag them."

Adie had a hundred things she wanted to know, but she kept quiet and held out her hands in front of her so that the footmen could tie them together, hoping that they wouldn't insist on tying them behind her back. This way, she'd feel more balanced and less likely to fall flat on her face on the uneven ground if they had a long march ahead of them. Happily, Elsie followed her lead and the footmen made quick work of their job.

The ropes the footmen used to bind their wrists seemed to be made from braided grasses, but they were no less strong for that. The sisters were led off under one of the big beech trees above Aunt Lillian's homestead, where they were kept under guard. The two girls sat down with their backs against the tree, leaning against each other as they listened to the conversation coming from where the queen and her court sat on their horses.

"Is there word on the girl yet?" the queen was saying. "The sooner we trade these sisters of hers for that wretched 'sangman, the happier I'll be."

"Not yet, madam," one of the other riders replied.

Before he could go on, a footman came running up.

"The 'sangmen have the older twins," he reported.

"Will she choose between the sisters?" the queen asked. "Does she fancy any above the others?"

"There's no way of telling."

"What about the younger twins?"

"We have scouts looking for them."

Elsie leaned closer to Adie, her mouth near her older sister's ear.

"What are they talking about?" she asked, her voice quieter than a breath.

Adie shrugged. She cast a glance to their nearest captors. When she saw they weren't paying that close attention to them, she whispered in Elsie's ear.

"I don't know," she said. "But it's beginning to sound like Janey's got us all caught up in something we have no business being mixed up in."

"Do you know what 'sangmen are?"

"Haven't a clue. But I'd guess they have something to do with 'sang."

"And Janey was going out to harvest some yester-day."

Adie gave a grim nod. "And it sounds as though these 'sangmen—whatever they are—have Laurel and Bess."

"What did she mean about choosing between sisters?"

"I guess they were hoping to trade us for someone Janey has, but now things have gotten complicated because the other side has the twins to trade."

"I don't get any of this. Janey would never hurt anyone, never mind capture someone the way these people have."

"I don't think they're people," Adie said.

Elsie sighed. "I was afraid you'd say something like that."

They broke off when the queen glanced in their direction. Adie returned her glare with an innocent look and the queen's attention turned away from her once more.

"Look," Elsie whispered.

She nodded at the apple tree that Root was still guarding. The fairies' dogs had formed a half circle around him, effectively penning him in. But Root paid no attention to them. His gaze stayed fixed on the tree in front of him like there wasn't a fairy court behind him.

Oh, why didn't you run off? Adie thought. You'll be no match for that many dogs and who knows what magical powers they have.

But oddly enough, the fairy dogs showed no inclination of doing more than keeping Root penned up against the apple tree. Adie wondered why. Perhaps it was only because the fairy queen hadn't given the order for them to attack yet. Then she returned her attention to the conversation of the queen and her courtiers and the answer came.

"Has *anyone* tracked down the girl yet?" the queen was asking.

There was a moment of silence before one of her court replied.

"No, madam. We only know she's with the Apple Tree Man, but we can't reach them because the dog's barring the way through Applejack's door and no one knows where it opens on the other side."

"Then remove the dog."

That command drew another silence. Apparently, Adie realized, no one liked to deliver bad news to their cranky queen.

"We can't," one of the riders said. "It won't meet our gaze."

Adie and Elsie exchanged glances.

"Does that mean what I think it does?" Elsie whispered.

Adie shrugged. She wasn't sure, but what it seemed the fairies were saying was that you had to acknowledge their presence before they could interact with you. So maybe if they just concentrated on not believing the fairy court was here...

Before she could go any further with that, the queen began to speak again.

"This should have been over long ago," she complained. "We should have had a dead 'sangman by now and moved on to other matters."

"But the princess...your daughter. The 'sangmen still have her."

"She's no longer my daughter," the queen said. "Not after she's soiled herself by loving a 'sangman. Let her live in the dirt with them and see how she likes it."

Now that was harsh, Adie thought. She could remember when she was a little girl, reading fairy tales
and watching Disney movies, how desperately she'd
wanted to meet a fairy. Unlike Janey, she'd long
grown out of that, but now she was happy she hadn't
gotten her wish back then. And would have been happier still not to be experiencing this. The fairy queen
was too much like an evil stepmother. But she supposed that was to be expected, considering the kind
of folklore that was told in these hills. Many of Aunt
Lillian's stories were downright gruesome.

Adie frowned, wishing she hadn't started this train
of thought.

Elsie pressed against her and whispered, "I think
we should try to follow Root's lead and, I don't know,
disbelieve in these horrible people."

It was worth a try, Adie supposed. Though she
could see it would be hard. Root might be able to fo-
cus entirely on one thing, but he was a dog and what
did he know? Dogs already had a one-track mind.
But she and Elsie had bound wrists to contend with.
Noisy captors, jingling bridles.

She was about to close her eyes and give it a try, but
the chance was gone.

A new commotion erupted on the far side of the fairy court. Adie craned her neck to see who had arrived, and her heart sank. Their arms and faces might have been covered in bees, but she had no trouble recognizing that it was Grace and Ruth who were under all those buzzing insects.

"This just gets worse and worse," Elsie moaned beside her.

Adie gave a slow nod.

CHAPTER FOURTEEN

Laurel and Bess

Laurel found herself wishing that she hadn't ignored Bess's common sense and simply left well enough alone. In fact, what she really wished was that they were back in the garden, doing their chores like they'd promised Mama they would. Doing chores would be way better than being here.

It was pitch dark and damp in the place the little man had brought them. Underground, she assumed, since the floor was dirt, as were the walls. She hadn't been able to reach up far enough to touch the ceiling.

"Don't fret," the little tree man had said before closing the door. "You won't be here long."

Easy enough for him to say.

She felt around in the dark until her fingers touched the sleeve of Bess's shirt.

"I'm sorry I didn't listen to you," she said.

"That's okay." Bess found Laurel's hand and gave it a squeeze. "I mean, it's not okay being here, but it's not your fault that he tricked us with his fairy music and changed our instruments into stones."

"If I hadn't been so greedy with that contest business—"

"He would have just found some other way to get us here."

"But still..."

"Still, nothing," Bess said. "There was some kind of magic spell in that music of his. It made my head go all fuzzy and probably did the same to you."

Laurel thought about that. She had felt all muddled for the first while, but now it was as though a fog had lifted and she felt more clearheaded than she had in hours.

"What do you think they're going to do to us?" she asked.

"I'm trying not to think about it," Bess said.

"I wish I'd stuck some of that garlic from the garden in my pocket. Or maybe we could make a cross."

Bess actually laughed. The sound of it made Laurel feel better, like maybe the end of the world wasn't quite here yet.

"You're thinking of vampires," Bess said.

"Well, what don't little tree men like?"

"Who knows? Fire, probably."

"Do you have any matches?"

"Sure. Right here in my pocket with my corncob pipe."

Laurel sighed. "That's okay. We haven't got anything to burn anyway."

Bess gave her hand another squeeze.

"We just have to be patient," she said, "and wait for our chance."

"And then we kick butt."

"I know I'd like to kick something."

A Savage Grace

CHAPTER FIFTEEN

Sarah Jane

*I*t was a funny thing about that world on the other side of the Apple Tree Man's door. You'd think that Aunt Lillian and I would be overwhelmed when we went through to the Otherworld, but it didn't happen that way.

Sure, the place was a shock to our senses. Colors were more intense...oh, what am I saying? *Everything* was more intense. The sharp colors, the crisp air we breathed, the lush texture of the grass, trilling birdsong drifting down from the trees, and an endless azure-blue sky above. But I remembered what the Apple Tree Man had told us about coming to this place—how we'd never want to leave, and I didn't feel that way at all.

When I said as much, the Apple Tree Man gave me a funny look. I thought maybe I'd offended him, so I tried to explain.

"When I was younger," I said, "we moved all the time, from one trailer park to another. It got so I never felt like I fit in, not anywhere we lived. I'm not blaming Mama and Daddy—that's just the way it was. Leastwise, it was until we moved to Granny Burrell's farm. Now I've lived there for pretty much as long as I've lived in all those other places put together, and you know what? I really like it.

"I like my familiar woods, watching the changes settle on them, season after season. I don't feel like a visitor anymore. I'm a neighbor now. I belong. And pretty as this place is, I don't belong here. I feel it like a buzz just under my skin. It's saying, 'You've got another home.'"

"You could've took the words right out of my mouth," Aunt Lillian said. "I remember how scared I was of those woods around the homestead when I first came to live with my aunt Em. But that feeling went away pretty quick and I've never wanted to leave them since. Even Paradise is going to seem wanting after living in those hills of ours."

The Apple Tree Man shook his head as he looked from her to me.

"I guess a body's never too old to be surprised," he said, "but I have to tell you, I had no idea you were so strong."

"Strong?" I said.

He nodded. "To resist the enchantments of this place so effortlessly."

"Makes you think, doesn't it?" Aunt Lillian said. "'Bout wasted years and all."

He nodded again, slower this time. I guess it finally hit him that he didn't have to keep Aunt Lillian at a distance—didn't have to, never had to. He got this hangdog look in his eyes that made me want to tell a joke or something, just to cheer him up.

"I just didn't know," he said.

"It's the red hair that makes them strong, Apple-jack," a voice said from above. "Why else do you think we cherish it so?"

Aunt Lillian and I fairly jumped out of our skins. We looked up and saw what we thought was a cat sitting up there on a branch, looking back down at us. Except it wasn't really a cat. It was more like a strange little cat man with a long tail and all covered with

black fur and catlike features. It had fingers like me, but a cat's retracting claws that were protruding at the moment as he cleaned them with a bright pink tongue.

"How come fairy creatures like to talk to me from out of trees?" Aunt Lillian said.

"What do you mean?" I asked.

"Nothing," she said. "It's an old story."

The cat man stretched out along his branch, head propped up on one hand. He looked to be about twice the height of our little unconscious 'sangman, but that still only made him a couple of feet tall.

"Oh, do tell," he said.

But Aunt Lillian had already looked away, her attention now on the Apple Tree Man.

"He called you Applejack," she said. "Is that your real name—the one you never told me?"

"It's a name," the Apple Tree Man said. "The one by which I'm known in this place, just like I'm the Apple Tree Man in your world."

"So what *is* your name?" I asked.

"Well, when he's drunk," the cat man said, "we call him Billy Cider."

"We don't have names the way you do," the Apple

Tree Man said. "We don't have any need for them. All we have are what people call us."

"Like sometimes," the cat man said, "people call me Li'l Pater." He waited a beat, then added, "You know, because I could be a smaller version of the Father of Cats."

Aunt Lillian looked back up at him and smiled. "A *much* smaller version," she said. "And not nearly as fierce."

He shrugged, then continued grooming his claws. "It's just what some people call me."

I got the feeling that this was something he tried out on every new person he met, hoping that they'd think maybe he really was kin to that big old black panther that Aunt Lillian had met when she was younger than me.

"We can call you that," I said.

"What are you doing here?" the Apple Tree Man asked.

Li'l Pater smiled. "I came to see the fireworks, and oh my, they should be something."

"Fireworks?" I asked.

"He doesn't mean actual fireworks," the Apple Tree Man explained.

"You do know that the bee queen's really unhappy with you?" Li'l Pater asked.

The Apple Tree Man sighed, then glanced at Aunt Lillian. "She'd better get in line."

"I'm not mad at you," Aunt Lillian told him. "Just disappointed you never took the chance."

"Why's the bee queen mad?" I asked.

"When isn't she mad?" Li'l Pater replied. "But this time it's because that little 'sangman you've got stowed away in that basket stole away her daughter, and you got in the middle of her settling her debt with him."

I looked at the Apple Tree Man. "I thought that happened ages ago."

"It did," Li'l Pater said before the Apple Tree Man could speak. "The *first* time. But this is the seventh daughter of hers that's gone off and wed a 'sangman. She was sure the sixth would be the last. But for good measure she kept this one in a hive as tall as a tree, locked up in a little room way up top with only a window to look out of."

"Like Rapunzel."

"Don't know her. What court is she from?"

"It's a tale in a storybook."

"This isn't a story," Li'l Pater said.

"What I don't understand," Aunt Lillian said, "is why these daughters of hers keep running off to marry 'sangmen. You say there've been seven now?"

"Just like me and my sisters," I said.

"You've *all* married 'sangmen?" Li'l Pater asked.

"No, I just meant there's seven of us, too."

Li'l Pater nodded. "Lucky number. 'Specially when you add in the red hair."

"What's so special about red hair?"

"Everything. A fairy can't hardly resist a red-haired human. It's as much a reason for them to be kidnapping your sisters as to make a bargain with you."

"Wait a minute. What do you mean, 'kidnapping' my sisters?"

Li'l Pater regarded us all with surprise. "You didn't know? The 'sangmen have two, and the bee court has the other four."

I thought my heart would stop in my chest. I gave Aunt Lillian and the Apple Tree Man an anguished look, but they only shook their heads in sympathy.

"Why...why are they doing this?" I asked the cat man.

"For barter," Li'l Pater said. "They want to trade your sisters for the 'sangman in your basket."

"But we were already *bringing* him back."

"They don't know that."

"And if both sides have my...my sisters...what am I supposed to do? Choose between who I'll save and who I'll sacrifice?" I looked down at the unconscious 'sangman. "For this little man that I don't even know?"

"Should have thought of that before you got involved," Li'l Pater said.

I nodded glumly. Aunt Lillian had warned me often enough. The one sure road to trouble, she'd say, is to get mixed up in the middle of a fairy quarrel.

"That doesn't matter now," I said. "All that's important is that we rescue my sisters, and for that, we need a plan."

"This should be good," Li'l Pater said, a distinctive purr in his voice.

"And to start with," I went on, "I don't want *you* around when I'm making it."

The purr stopped. "What did I ever—"

"I don't know you," I told him. "And right now I can't take the chance of trusting you." I turned to the Apple Tree Man. "And come to think of it, who's to say that I can trust you, either?"

"Now, Sarah Jane," Aunt Lillian said, "the Apple Tree Man might be a lot of things, but—"

I shook my head, not letting her finish. "He may be your friend, but I wouldn't call him a very good one. And he certainly hasn't said or done anything to prove that he's mine. I won't take the chance of trusting any fairy—not with my sisters' lives at stake."

Before anyone could protest, I stepped over to where the Apple Tree Man had set down the basket with the 'sangman still sleeping in it. I picked up the basket.

"I may have my own disappointments with the Apple Tree Man," Aunt Lillian said, "but I'd trust him with my very life."

"What about the lives of my sisters?"

She regarded me for a long moment, then shook her head.

"I've told you what's true for me," she said, "but only you can decide who *you* should trust."

I didn't know where this fierce feeling had come from—probably some protective reflex locked in the Dillard genes. We were the kind of folks who depended on ourselves. But blind panic also coursed through my veins, born out of the shock of learning that my sisters were in danger and it was my fault. My fault, but fairies were caught up in every which part of it.

The Apple Tree Man was a fairy being. Could he really be trusted?

The thing that finally swayed me was how the Apple Tree Man didn't try to change my mind. Li'l Pater sat up on his branch, obviously insulted and muttering to himself. I wasn't listening to him. But the Apple Tree Man stood calmly waiting for me to make up my own mind.

And I guess the other thing that swayed me was that I didn't have the first clue as to how to proceed. I didn't know where the 'sangmen lived—leastways, not in this world. I didn't know what to do when I found them. I also knew nothing about these bee fairies or how to go about rescuing my sisters from them. I was pretty much stuck.

So I took a breath and looked at the Apple Tree Man.

"I'm sorry," I said. "If Aunt Lillian trusts you that much, I should be able to do the same. I'm just so worried about my sisters."

"I understand," he said.

"And what about me?" Li'l Pater asked, grumblings forgotten. "Are you going to let me help?" He grinned and spread his fingers and his cat claws popped out from the end of each of them. "I can be fierce as the Father himself."

Having accepted the Apple Tree Man's help, I looked to him for guidance on this. He gave Li'l Pater a stern look.

"Promise you'll only help?" he asked. "No tricks, no jokes?"

Li'l Pater stretched and nodded.

"You swear on the fangs of the Father?"

The cat man's eyes opened wider and he nodded again.

The Apple Tree Man turned back to me.

"By that oath," he said, "you can trust him."

"So what do we do?" I asked.

I was anxious. I didn't know what the fairies were

doing to my sisters, but every moment they were with them was far too long for me.

"First we'll follow our original plan," the Apple Tree Man said. "We'll visit the 'sangmen and free the sisters they have. When they realize that we're returning their little prince, they'll be honor-bound to let your sisters go and help us."

"And the bee fairies?" Aunt Lillian asked.

"I have an idea about how to deal with them, though it will depend on Sarah Jane's courage."

The very idea of bees made my knees knock, but I resolved to try whatever needed to be done.

CHAPTER SIXTEEN

Adie and Elsie

Adie and Elsie watched the meadow from their spot by the beech tree, where their guards had brought them. The attention of the whole fairy court, including their guards, was on a tubby little man who approached the queen with Ruth and Grace in tow.

They were still some distance away, but so far, other than being covered in bees, the twins didn't seem to be hurt. As Adie and Elsie watched, the entire swarm of bees coating their sisters rose up and flew to the queen. They hovered for a moment, then disappeared into the folds of her gown, patterning it as though they were woven into the fabric.

Adie turned her attention to Elsie's knapsack. The fairies had left it on her back, either because they didn't know what it was, or they didn't care. After all, what could a couple of girls do, hands bound and with such a host to stand against them?

"What do you use to sharpen those pencils of yours?" Adie asked.

"Just this old jackknife that George gave me," Elsie said.

"Is it sharp?"

"Well, sure it is. It has to be to shave the wood properly...." Her voice trailed off and she gave Adie a quick look. "What are you planning to do with it?"

"Whatever it takes to rescue the twins and get us all out of here."

Adie looked again at the scene in the meadow. All the bee fairies remained fascinated with what was going on. If she was ever going to have a chance, this was it.

"Turn around so I can get at your knapsack," she said.

"Oh, I don't like this," Elsie said, but she turned as asked, whispering, "There's too many of them, Adie."

"I only need to get to the queen," Adie replied.

With bound hands, Adie had trouble getting the knapsack's drawstring undone, but she finally got it loose and was able to reach in. She dug awkwardly among Elsie's sketchbooks and the various roots, twigs, and whatnots until she felt the handle of the jackknife and pulled it out. Laying it on the ground, she took a moment to close up the knapsack again before trying to open the knife. After much fussing and one broken nail, she managed to pry the blade out of the handle and began the awkward process of sawing through the grass rope binding Elsie's hands. Luckily, Elsie hadn't been exaggerating. The blade was sharp and sliced easily through.

"Here. Now do mine," Adie said.

Elsie hesitated. "This is only asking for more trouble," she said.

"Come on, Elsie. They brought it on."

Elsie checked again to make sure that they were still unobserved, then sliced through the ropes binding her sister's wrists and passed the knife back to Adie.

"So you're just going to stab her?" Elsie asked, a horrified look on her face.

"Look," Adie said. "They're not even people, okay? They're like bugs. And when bugs start annoying you, you squash them."

"But—"

"Look what they've done to our Ruthie and Grace," Adie said. "No one threatens my sisters, Elsie. That's the bottom line. Now put your hands back together."

Adie arranged the cut ropes back on top of Elsie's wrists. "Make sure you keep your hands in your lap, like they're still tied."

Elsie nodded, her nervous glance returning to where the twins were being brought up to the bee fairy queen.

"Let me try to put the ropes back on yours," she said to Adie.

"No need. I'm going to slip off into the woods. What I want you to do is create a diversion in about, say, five minutes."

Elsie stared at her in horror. "I'd rather try the disbelieving business first."

Adie shook her head. "It's way too late for that. I mean, we *know* they're here, right?"

"I suppose."

"Trust me on this," Adie said.

Before Elsie could think of something else to try to get her to stay, Adie slipped off behind the beech tree and into the woods.

CHAPTER SEVENTEEN

Laurel and Bess

"I think I hate the dark," Laurel said.

"This is the first I've heard of it," Bess's voice replied.

"Maybe I've always hated it, but I just didn't know till now because I was never anyplace so dark before."

Normally, all Laurel had to do was close her eyes and she could call up Bess's features in her mind's eye. But here, where it was black as coal whether she had her eyes open or not, she couldn't do it. There was only the unending dark and it was getting to her.

"If we were Girl Scouts," she went on, "we'd have come prepared with a flashlight."

She couldn't see Bess's smile, but she could feel it.

"Or at least a candle and matches," Bess said.

"Exactly. And maybe a bag of chips or some cookies."

"Except, if we were Girl Scouts," Bess said, "we'd still be working in the garden, because Girl Scouts do what they say they'll do. They don't go chasing off after fiddlers in the woods."

"So we'd be lousy Girl Scouts from the get-go."

"Pretty much."

Laurel sighed. "I guess we should have been looking out for some little old lady to help on our way into the woods. Or a talking spoon. Or a lion with a thorn in his paw or something."

"What for?"

"Well, you know. In the stories they always come back to help you when you get in a pickle."

"I hate stories like that," Bess said. "People should help each other just for the sake of doing a kind deed— not because they're scared not to, or for some reward."

"You mean like Sarah Jane helps Aunt Lillian."

Now it was Bess's turn to sigh. "And we're always teasing her about it. I guess you're right. We should have been looking for talking spoons and the like."

"Nobody even knows we're here, do they?" Laurel said.

"Except for the little man who dumped us here."

Neither said anything for a long moment.

"Did I mention how much I hate the dark?" Laurel finally asked.

"Maybe once."

Laurel squeezed Bess's hand. If she had to be stuck in a place like this, there was no one else she'd rather be with. This was how they came into the world, the two of them, together in the dark womb. Perhaps they were going to go out in the darkness as well. That made her think about her life and what she'd done with it. Sarah Jane had a few years' worth of good deeds in her favor. What did she have?

"So, do you think we're shallow people?" she asked.

"No," Bess said. "We're passionate about music, aren't we? I don't think that shallow people are passionate about anything."

"Music. That's what got us here in the first place. There was some kind of magic in that fiddling, wasn't there? You knew right away, didn't you?"

"I didn't know, exactly," Bess said. "But I knew something wasn't right." Laurel thought Bess was finished, but after a moment Bess added, "Maybe we should make our own magic music."

"With what? We don't have any instruments."

"We could lilt a tune."

"And do what with it?" Laurel asked. "If you've been taking magic lessons, this is the first I've heard of it."

"Well, at least it would help to pass the time."

"That's true."

They both fell quiet until Laurel finally said, "I can't think of a single tune."

"This from the girl who was ready to have a tune contest with a woody fairy man."

"I can't believe I was so stupid."

"You weren't stupid," Bess said. "You were enchanted. It's not the same thing."

"I suppose. Oh, I know. We could try that version of 'Walk Like an Egyptian' that we never got to play at the dance last night."

"I don't know. I think it'd be too hard without my banjo. How about 'Sourwood Mountain' instead?"

"Okay."

Bess started to hum the tune. When Laurel came in with a high "diddly-diddly" lilting, Bess joined her, the two of them taking turns harmonizing on the melody. They went from tune to tune, sticking with those that were associated with the Stanley Brothers, since that was how they'd started, and it was as though they were sitting in on a session with instruments in hand. Everything went away, except for the music. It didn't particularly help them in their present situation, but it did make them feel better.

CHAPTER EIGHTEEN

Sarah Jane

I let Aunt Lillian and the Apple Tree Man take the lead and followed behind with Li'l Pater at my side. The little cat man still seemed put out that I hadn't wanted to include him in our party and wasn't speaking to me, but that was okay. I didn't really want to talk to anybody. I didn't want to talk, didn't want to think. I just wanted my sisters to be safe again.

The only thing that made any of this even remotely bearable was seeing how well Aunt Lillian and the Apple Tree Man were getting along. It was as though she'd shed a whole mess of years—her back was straighter, and she had a spring in her step and was giggling. Maybe it was something in the air of this place, but more likely it had to do with the fact that the Apple Tree Man was finally back in her life.

Personally, I don't know what she saw in him. Now, he wasn't butt-ugly, but he sure wasn't going to win himself any prizes for handsomeness, either. I guess it's that he just wasn't human, not with his gnarly limbs and that barky skin with all those twigs and leaves and such growing out of him every which where. I'd have thought that maybe at Aunt Lillian's age, courting wasn't so important anymore, but she was acting just like Adie or the older twins do when they're flirting with some fellow.

"How come you're so mad at me?" Li'l Pater said.

I turned to him. "What?"

"Well, you must be, the way you're giving me the silent treatment and all."

I didn't really want to be talking about this with him, but I supposed it would be a distraction from worrying about my sisters.

"I'm not mad at you," I said. "I don't even know you."

"And that's why you don't want my help."

"Look," I told him. "The Apple Tree Man vouches for you, and Aunt Lillian vouches for him, so here we all are."

"But you don't want me to be here, do you?"

"I just want my sisters to be safe."

"We'll rescue them," he said with a confidence I didn't feel. "We're in the middle of a story now and since we're the heroes, it has to all come out right for us in the end. You'll see."

"Except in *their* minds, the bee fairies and 'sangmen are the heroes. Who's to say that the story won't go their way?"

"I never thought about that."

"Well, don't," I told him, already regretting that I'd put the notion in his head. Mama often said that putting bad thoughts into the air by speaking them aloud was a sure way to call bad luck to you. "I like the way you think it'll all work out."

I was so busy talking to Li'l Pater that I bumped right into the Apple Tree Man, never having realized that he and Aunt Lillian had come to a stop.

"What is it?" I asked.

But I guessed pretty quickly, by the stony ground underfoot and the thick canopy of poplar and beech and oak. We were on familiar ground, standing at the top of a slope running down into a 'sang field, the plants growing thick and tall below us. We could have been in the same one that I found the 'sangman in yesterday. I suppose some places aren't that much different from one world to the other.

"I'm going to call the 'sangmen to us," the Apple Tree Man said. "Unless they ask you a question directly, let me do the talking."

I gave him a reluctant nod, still not trusting him as much as Aunt Lillian apparently did.

"And if you do have to answer a question," he added, "give them the answer and nothing more."

"Do you know these people?" I asked.

"We've met, but I've never spent much time with them. I don't cotton to the whole idea of courts and royalty and all the way some of the fairies do."

"Why not?"

"Well, the trouble with courts," the Apple Tree Man said, "is you're stuck with a king or a queen, and they almost always think that the whole world turns around them."

I knew a few folks like that back in our own world.

"I like to go my own way," he added, "and not be beholden to anyone else."

I knew a bunch of folks like that, too, starting with pretty much my whole family.

"I'll follow your lead," I told him.

He called out, making a sound that was like a cross between the nasal *yank-yank* of a nuthatch and a fox's bark. I gave Aunt Lillian a look, but she was studying the land below. When I turned to have my own look at the 'sang field, I saw them come popping up all over the patch, little 'sangmen and women, all gnarled and rooty like the wounded fellow I'd rescued—the one that had gotten us all into this mess in the first place.

It was eerie to watch. One minute there was just the 'sang, growing taller and with more prongs than I'd ever seen back in our own world, and the next we had a whole mess of these little people in among the 'sang, and not much taller than the plants, looking up at us. It was like they'd sprouted right up out of the ground and, for all I knew, that's exactly what they did.

But what concerned me just then was how there wasn't one of them wearing what I'd call a friendly expression. I looked to the Apple Tree Man and didn't take much comfort from the fact that he didn't seem near so worried as I was feeling my ownself. I started to say something, but then I remembered his warning. So I just stood there and kept my mouth

shut, waiting along with the others as those 'sangfolk came up the slope toward us.

Oh, it was a strange sight. A goodly number of them were taller than the little man I'd found—two or three times his one-foot height, some of them. But the lot of them looked pretty much the same, more tree than man. They were like walking bushes with bark for skin and rooty hair, and twigs and leaves and everysuch growing up out of them every which place you might look.

The one in front was near four feet high, but something made him seem bigger still. I can't tell you exactly what it was. Maybe it was the fact that he was the boss, which was something I found out as soon as he and the Apple Tree Man began to talk.

"So, Applejack," this big 'sangman said. "Have you come to trade my boy's life for the two girls?"

The Apple Tree Man shook his head. When he spoke, his voice was mild, with just the smallest hint of a rebuke in it.

"We were merely bringing him back to you," he said. "Doing what any good neighbor would do when he sees someone in trouble."

I felt Li'l Pater stiffen at my side and knew what he was thinking. The Apple Tree Man had just up

and given away our bargaining chip. But I guess I'd have done the same if I were him. There's no time when it's right to trade in people's lives, no ifs or buts about it. Though, if you want to look for a silver lining, I suppose it's always better to have somebody be beholden to you than not.

But I still held my breath, waiting for that 'sangman king to answer. After all, these were my sisters we were talking about.

"Looks like I owe you an apology," the king finally said. "I was told you were ready to trade him to the bee court, but I should have known better."

The Apple Tree Man didn't reply. He just handed over that basket as easy as you please. A 'sangwoman came up from behind the king and plucked the boy out of the basket. The way she held him so close to her chest, I figured she had to be his mother. 'Bout then I also noticed this pretty little thing, as different from the 'sangmen as I am from a crow. She was pale-skinned and golden-haired, her features fine and sharp, and fluttering at her back were a pair of honest-to-goodness little wings.

She came sidling up and the 'sangwoman included her in her embrace.

"Someone bring up those red-haired girls," the king said over his shoulder.

One of the other bigger 'sangmen popped out of sight and before you could say Jimmy-had-a-penny, he was back with Laurel and Bess in tow. The two of them stood blinking in the sun, Bess brushing dirt from her jeans.

Soon as I saw them, I didn't mind me either the Apple Tree Man's advice or the worry of maybe upsetting the 'sangman. I just ran forward and hugged them both, as relieved to see them, I reckon, as the 'sang queen was to get her own boy back.

We were still in the middle of all that when the king started in with the tall tales, trying to cover up for how he hadn't trusted that the Apple Tree Man, at least, would do right by him and his people. I guess royalty in fairyland isn't all that much different from the politicians in ours. Folks in charge just can't seem to actually admit to making a mistake and you can't really call them on their lies because, as soon as the words leave their mouths, it's gospel, so far as they're concerned.

"We aren't like the bee queen," he said. "We took the girls, sure, but only to protect them. When we heard that the bees had captured two of your young miss's sisters, I sent my forester to watch out for any others and protect them, should they happen to come into Tanglewood Forest.

"These two did and he brought them here safe. But when he got back to watching for more, it was too late. Word was, yet another pair had been captured by the bees."

"What's that?" Laurel demanded, turning toward me, as did Bess.

"Is he...talking about our Ruthie and Grace?" asked Bess, wringing her hands.

"Looks like," I said. "We've got to find a way to rescue the girls. They've all been taken by bee fairies."

"*Bee* fairies?" both twins said at once.

"Yes. Let's see what we can do about it." I led the twins over to where Aunt Lillian was standing with the Apple Tree Man. They gave Li'l Pater a curious look, but by then they must have been getting as used to the notion of fairy-tale people as I was, and they were more interested in what the king was saying. Laurel hadn't heard the Apple Tree Man's warning about letting him do the talking, and I guess, being Laurel, she probably wouldn't have listened anyway.

Laurel stomped her foot on the ground. "That fiddling fairyman wasn't just watching out for us," she spat. "He pulled us right into the forest with his fiddle playing and that tricksy contest of his."

"What else was I supposed to do?" the forester said.

I recognized him as the 'sangman who'd brought the twins up from wherever it was they'd been held. I was surprised to find myself starting to tell the difference between the 'sangmen because when they first came popping up all over the 'sang field, I'd have said they all looked the same.

"*You* try sitting in a meadow for hour after hour," he went on, "waiting on the chance that somebody might or might not take it into their head to come rambling up in the woods. You'd want to play your fiddle, too, to pass the time."

"But you put some kind of spell on us with your music."

He shook his head. "As I said, I was just passing the time."

"And your 'contest'?"

"I thought it a good way to bring you back without having to go into all the whys and wherefores, which you probably wouldn't have believed anyway."

"Right. So then you turned our instruments into rocks and—"

"Now that's just a plain lie!"

"Now, everybody, hold on," the king said. "Maybe we didn't choose the best way to bring you here—"

"Not to mention that the accommodations were awful," Laurel muttered.

"—but we meant well."

I didn't much care what he said. He could tell any kind of story at all so far as I was concerned, so long as Laurel and Bess were safe. But my sisters weren't ready to let it go just yet.

"Then who stole our instruments?" Bess asked.

"Maybe we can worry on that later," the Apple Tree Man said. "Right now we should be making plans to rescue your other sisters."

"We can't field the same numbers as the bee court," the king said, "but we'll fight alongside you until we win or there's none of us left standing."

"I was hoping to find a more peaceful way to settle this," the Apple Tree Man said.

I nodded in agreement, but the king shook his head.

"The bees only know one kind of argument—who's stronger," he told us.

"Maybe so," the Apple Tree Man said, "and I don't mind having you to fall back on if things don't go right. But I've got something else I'd like to try first."

Turned out we were pretty much all in disagreement with the Apple Tree Man's strange plan when he was done telling it, except for Li'l Pater, who I still wasn't sure was really on our side. The Apple Tree Man was helping us on account of Aunt Lillian, and the 'sang-men were because they felt beholden to us, but Li'l Pater remained a mystery.

"You've trusted me so far," the Apple Tree Man said. "Trust me just a little longer."

"And if your plan doesn't work?" I asked, not wanting to think of what might happen to my sisters, but finding it impossible to ignore my fears.

"No one will be hurt," he said.

"Can you *promise* me that?"

He hesitated for a long moment, then slowly shook his head. "Can't anybody promise you that."

"It'll work," Li'l Pater assured us. "The one thing fairies can't resist is a mystery."

"Never did much trust all the darn cats in these woods," muttered Laurel.

⌒

In the end, we agreed to try the Apple Tree Man's plan. By all accounts, the bee court far outnumbered the 'sangmen, and adding in us three girls, the Apple Tree Man, an old woman, and a little cat man didn't seem to change the odds much in our favor. But since no one could come up with a better idea, we were stuck with this one, for better or worse.

"You're not doing this alone, Janey," Bess said.

Laurel nodded in agreement.

"But—"

"They're our sisters, too."

I looked to Aunt Lillian and the Apple Tree Man for support, but didn't find any.

"If there are three of you, it'll work more in your favor," he said. "Especially since you're all red-haired."

"What's that got to do with anything?" Bess asked.

"Redheads are sacred to the Father of Cats," Li'l Pater explained. "Most fairies won't harm them."

"So we don't really have anything to worry about,"

I said, happy now to have endured all those years of being called "carrottop," "freckleface," and the like in the schoolyard.

The Apple Tree Man got an uncomfortable look.

"I said 'most,'" Li'l Pater told us.

"And there are many ways to hurt a person," the king of the 'sangmen added, "without actually killing them."

"Great," Laurel said.

Bess nodded glumly. "Yes, that's *really* comforting to hear."

The thought of anything bad happening to my sisters was too much for me to be able to hold in my head for long without going crazy.

"Let's just get on with it," I said.

CHAPTER NINETEEN

Ruth and Grace

The worst thing, Grace thought, about having bees all over your face and arms was how they tickled. But you didn't dare do a thing about it. All you could do was feel the way your skin squirmed under all those fuzzy little bee feet and try not to sneeze or swat at them and their tiny riders. It was horrible.

Even when the cloud of bees finally lifted from her and Ruth, she could still sense thousands of little feet carpeting her skin. It was like how you still feel cobwebs clinging to you after you've brushed them away. You know they're gone, but a ghostly veil of them still clings to your skin.

"Grace...?" Ruth said at her side.

Instead of rubbing at her face and arms the way Grace was, Ruth was staring past Grace, farther up the slope, her face pale. Grace slowly turned to see what had caught her sister's attention.

She almost wished she hadn't.

Bee fairies, it seemed, could come in any size. From the tiny ones that had covered them on the journey to get here and the fat bumblebee man who'd captured them, to these terrifying lords and the lady with their grim faces, sitting tall and straight-backed on horses that didn't seem quite right. But then the riders weren't quite right, either. They were almost people, but their features were all too sharp and they had a cold light in their eyes like no normal person Grace had ever seen. There were footmen, too. A lot of them, all armed with bows and arrows, rapiers, and slender spears with barbed tips.

Her own heart sank.

"So," she said in a small voice, her hand reaching for and finding Ruth's. "Tell me again why we left the house today, when we could have been safely doing housework, which, I have to tell you now, I would just love to be doing because it'd sure beat being here."

"Anything would beat being here," Ruth said.

"You wouldn't happen to have any firecrackers in your pocket, would you? Or a pistol, say?"

"No, but...but would a can of Raid do?"

Grace squeezed her hand and found a weak smile. *Never let them see you're scared,* she remembered Adie telling them once, when she and Ruth were being picked on by some kids at school. *Fear only eggs them on like a pack of dogs. Just stand up and take the licking, and try to give back as good as you get. You might get hurt, but they're going to know you're not easy targets and next time they'll think twice before they come after you.*

And it had worked, too—a couple of black eyes and a few dozen scrapes and bruises later. They'd only ever had to fight twice, standing back-to-back as the bullies ganged up on them. After that, even the older kids left them alone.

"A can of Raid would be perfect," she told Ruth now.

"If only."

"And it would have to be humongous. How big a pocket do you have, anyway?"

"Be still!" the only woman in the group told them. She looked to be their leader—the queen bee,

Grace supposed. They all had a hardness—a mean, savage air about them, but from the look of her, she could have invented the very idea of meanness. Which was awful for a whole bunch of reasons, but one was that she could have been so pretty if she hadn't let that cruelty twist her features.

Grace swallowed hard. No fear, she reminded herself. Or at least don't show it.

"Oh, shut up, yourself," she said. "Who do you think you are—our mother?"

Ruth tugged at her sleeve with her free hand. "You know, maybe we shouldn't be quite so—"

"I am hardly your mother," the woman interrupted, her voice like ice. "I am no one's mother. Not any longer."

"Big surprise there," Grace said. "No boyfriend, either, I'm guessing. Not with that personality."

"May-maybe you should think about a makeover," Ruth said.

That was the spirit, Grace thought.

"Oh sure," she added. "Mama says they can make you feel like a whole new woman, which, with you, would be a big improvement."

The woman's lips twisted into a gruesome smile,

which made her even scarier than when she was just looking mean.

If she could have, Grace would have taken off right then. Just run off with Ruth, as fast and far away from here as they could. But they couldn't outrun horses. Or those strange dogs she now spied, six or seven of them crouched in a half circle. She blinked, realizing that the dogs had Root penned up against the trunk of some old apple tree, though Root didn't appear to be taking much notice of them.

Turning back to the woman, she caught a glimpse of red hair farther up the slope. Staring harder, she realized it was Elsie, sitting on the ground under a big beech tree, her hands tied in front of her.

Did that mean they had Adie, too? And Janey?

"I don't know if you're brave or simply half-witted," the woman said, "and frankly, I don't care. But you are an annoyance."

"Shall we bind them and put them with the others?" one of the footmen standing by her horse asked.

"Well, now," the queen said. "We certainly don't need all four of these wretched girls to bargain with. All we need is one more than the dirt-eaters have."

"Should I take the other back to their world?" the fat little man who'd captured them asked.

"Why bother? Just kill one of them"—she gestured with her chin—"this rude one who talks too much—and put the other with her sisters."

"But, madam," the little man began, obviously as shocked as Grace was by the queen's offhand order for her execution. "They are red-haired...."

The queen gave him a long, cold look. "Are you arguing with me?"

"No, but...the Father of Cats says such mortals are sacred."

The queen made a sharp motion with her hand and one of the footmen stepped forward, notched an arrow and let it fly.

All of Grace's bravery fled. She winced, but the arrow wasn't meant for her. The little man went down, knees buckling under him. He gasped, tearing at the arrow with his fingers. Blood streamed over his hands and down his chest before he toppled over onto the ground.

Grace thought she was going to throw up. Ruth's sudden tight grip on her hand would have hurt if she weren't already gripping Ruth's hand just as fiercely.

"Well done," the queen told the archer. She turned to regard her court. "Does anyone else wish to question my orders?"

It had been quiet in the meadow before this. Now the silence was profound. Not even the horses moved.

The queen returned her gaze to the twins, that terrible smile twitching the corners of her mouth.

"That's better," she said. "Now if someone would deal with these little wretches…?"

The bowman notched another arrow.

CHAPTER TWENTY

Adie

reeping through the underbrush, Adie heard none of the twins' exchange with the queen. She was too busy sneaking up on one of the queen's footmen—a scout or a guard, she wasn't sure which. It didn't matter. All she knew was that she didn't want him behind her when she went for the queen with Elsie's jackknife.

She didn't really think she'd succeed. Or if she did, she doubted that she'd survive. But the jackknife was made of steel, so it had iron in it, and all the fairy tales said iron was deadly to fairies, so there was at least a chance that she'd be able to do some damage. And while she might not survive, perhaps her sisters might escape in the confusion.

That was all that really mattered. That they were safe.

Right now the jackknife was folded up in the pocket of her jeans. In her hands was a three-foot-long branch that she'd picked up under the trees. It hadn't been her first choice. She'd kept selecting and hefting various branches as she continued to sneak up on the bee fairy until she finally found one with enough weight that it didn't feel as though it would break on the first strike.

It was hard to stay quiet. If this part of the wood hadn't been sprucy-pine, she probably would have been noticed by now, but the ground was thick with a carpet of needles, spongy and silent underfoot. Every time she did make some noise—stepped on a twig, pushed through the occasional bush—she stopped and crouched low, not daring to breathe, hoping the bee fairy would think it was only a squirrel or bird.

Maybe it was true that the Dillards had some Indian blood in them, she thought as she managed to creep almost up on the footman without his noticing her.

Okay, this was it.

She straightened up, took a long, deep breath, and stepped forward, swinging the branch. The branch connected with the back of his head and he grunted, toppling forward, his spear falling from his hand. The footman landed on his hands, down, but not out. The force of her blow stung the palms of Adie's hands enough that she almost lost her grip on the branch. The footman was already half rising and turning in her direction.

They're not people, Adie reminded herself. They're nasty stinging insects. It's hurt them or be hurt *by* them.

Just as he was about to call out for help, she swung the branch again and caught him in the temple. This time he went down and lay still.

Adie dropped the branch and had to go down on one knee. She was shaking so hard she didn't think she could stand. Bile rose in her throat, but she made herself take a few steadying breaths until the queasiness passed and she was able to get back on her feet. Picking up her stick, she held it ready and nudged the footman with her foot. He remained motionless. She tried again. When he still didn't move, she switched her branch for his spear and began to work her way back to the meadow where the fairy court held her sisters captive.

She arrived just in time to see one of the queen's footmen kill a fat little man who looked like a bumble-bee, then aim his bow in Grace's direction.

CHAPTER TWENTY-ONE

Elsie

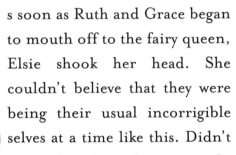

s soon as Ruth and Grace began to mouth off to the fairy queen, Elsie shook her head. She couldn't believe that they were being their usual incorrigible selves at a time like this. Didn't they know that they were only making things worse?

And speaking of things getting worse, any moment now, the bee fairies were going to notice that Adie was gone.

Checking that nobody was looking in her direction, she got to her feet and looked around for something that she could use as a weapon. She wished her legs didn't feel like jelly, that her heart wasn't lodged in her throat. That she could take at least one deep breath.

Why couldn't she be as brave as Adie, just getting up and doing what needed to be done?

She glanced back at the fairy court, then watched in horror as the queen had one of her footmen shoot the fat little man standing by the twins. The queen gave a second order and he notched another arrow and aimed it at Grace.

Elsie's protective instincts sent a surge of adrenaline through her so that she could move again. There was no time to worry if Adie was in position or not. Now was the time for the diversion. But just as she was trying to decide between running around shrieking like a madwoman or picking up a stick and attacking her captors, Sarah Jane, Laurel, and Bess suddenly came dancing into the glade, paying no attention to the gathering of bee fairies.

CHAPTER TWENTY-TWO

Sarah Jane

I felt like a guerrilla soldier as we made our way toward where the bee fairy court held my sisters captive. Li'l Pater led the way, which didn't particularly thrill me, but both the Apple Tree Man and the 'sangmen deferred to him in this, explaining that moving between the worlds could be tricky. The Apple Tree Man only went back and forth through his tree, while the 'sangmen crossed between their 'sang patches in either world. So without someone like Li'l Pater, we might end up miles from where we needed to be, or at a disadvantage as we all tried to sneak out of the Apple Tree Man's tree without being seen.

Li'l Pater brought us out of the fairies' world and

back into our own—right in the woods above Aunt Lillian's orchard. At one point he held up a hand for us to stop while he crept ahead. When he finally waved at us to follow, I spied one of the bee fairies unconscious behind a tree, trussed up with grass ropes. It seemed Li'l Pater was fiercer than you'd think from the size of him.

And then I saw the bee court and my sisters in the meadow below and realized he'd played us fair in this as well.

"I guess I misjudged you," I told him.

He was pretty gracious about it, except for a little smirk in one corner of his mouth.

"Oh, that's all right," he said. "I know you big folks can't help being the way you are."

"Yes, well, it's not like we—"

"You'll be careful," Aunt Lillian whispered, crouching beside us.

I nodded, wondering if she'd interrupted to stop me and Li'l Pater from getting into another argument. Probably. Not much got past Aunt Lillian. And though I was trying my best to hold my tongue, Li'l Pater didn't make it easy.

I turned from them to stare out at the bee fairies.

They were more like the way I'd always pictured fairies in my head—sort of special and scary, all at once.
Where the 'sangmen were all rooty and earthy, the
bee fairies were bright and shining, sharp-featured
and tall. Some rode horses, and they had a pack of
lean dogs that had Root penned up against the Apple
Tree Man's tree.

Root wasn't paying any attention to them. He was
just staring at that tree—waiting for us to come back
out again, I guess.

Looking back toward the fairy court, I picked out
the red heads of my sisters. Grace and Ruth were easy
to spot—they looked like they'd just been brought in
and were the center of everybody's attention. It took
me a little longer to find Elsie, up higher by a beech
tree. I couldn't see Adie, and my heart started racing.
I had to hope she was just lying down in the grass, out
of sight.

While I was studying the fairy court, the 'sangmen
slipped away from us, taking up positions all along
the edge of the woods, close to where we'd arrived.
They carried stout cudgels and spears, knives and
short bows with arrows made of some kind of dark
wood and fletched with what looked like owl feathers.

The 'sangmen would be our backup if the Apple Tree Man's plan didn't work out.

Seeing the size of the bee court, I was surely hoping it wouldn't come to a fight. There were *way* too many of the bee fairies for my liking.

Taking a steadying breath, I turned to Laurel and Bess.

"Remember," I warned them as we were about to leave our hidey-hole on the edge of the meadow. "No matter what happens, not a word."

Bess mimed a zipper closing from one corner of her mouth to the other.

"Hey," Laurel asked the Apple Tree Man. "Is it okay if we hum while we're doing this?"

"I don't see why not," he told them.

"And we could dance, too," Bess said, "till we get up close."

Laurel nodded. "But something slow. I vote for 'Shenandoah.'"

"Incongruous dancing is an excellent way to get their attention," the Apple Tree Man assured them.

"What do you think, Janey?" Laurel asked, turning to me.

"Why not?" I said.

Nothing seemed real anyway.

I looked away from them, back toward the bee court. The queen looked angry. She said something that I couldn't quite hear from where we were. But then she slashed her arm in a downward direction and one of her footmen just up and shot an arrow into the throat of a fat little man standing by the twins. My stomach lurched as he dropped to the ground, blood pouring out of his neck.

Suddenly the bowman had another arrow notched and was aiming it straight at Grace.

"Oh, please, no," I said. "Let's go. Now."

I turned to Laurel and Bess. Their tomfoolery had drained away along with the blood in their faces.

We were all feeling a little shaky as we came dancing our way out of the trees, Laurel and Bess humming that old tune in two-part harmony, all of us with handfuls of grass in one fist, the pieces cut to lengths of six or seven inches.

Please, please, please, I silently prayed. Let this work. Don't let them shoot Grace like they did that little man.

The bee court spotted us and a soft buzzing murmur arose, but I didn't dare look at them. I just concentrated on what I was doing, trying to be strange, dramatic, and graceful all at once. I wasn't nearly so nimble on my feet as the twins beside me, but I did my best.

Laurel and Bess got right into it, accustomed as they were to being onstage, performing in front of an audience, though I guess they'd never been in front of one this strange before. Compared to them I felt like a klutz, but I could take the embarrassment if it rescued my sisters.

About halfway between the trees and the bee court, we started laying down our blades of grass. We did it with deliberation, like it had meaning, just the way the Apple Tree Man had told us.

"Doesn't matter *what* it is you do," he'd said, "just so long as it's long past curious and you do it with conviction. And don't answer them when they ask what you're doing—just keep at it."

"But what if they get mad at us?"

"Oh, they'll get mad all right. But so long as you keep at it, they won't be able to help themselves. They'll just have to know what you're doing. Maybe they'll threaten you, maybe they'll threaten your sisters, but you stick it out. There'll come a point when they'll start bribing you with anything and everything you might imagine."

"I've got a pretty good imagination," Laurel said.

Bess poked her in the side, but she smiled.

"You hold on," the Apple Tree Man told us, "until they offer you a boon—that's the only time you stop and look straight at them."

So that's what we did. I could feel a terrible twitch up between my shoulder blades. I kept expecting that bowman to turn from Grace and shoot his arrow at one of us instead.

⌒

Anywise, like I said, halfway between them and the woods, we started making those patterns with the blades of grass, laying them on the ground, carefully studying what we'd done, then laying another. Nothing that made sense, but we acted like it was the most important thing in the world, and I suppose it was, considering what all was at stake.

I didn't look at the bee court, but I could hear them murmuring as I laid another blade of grass down, looked at it for a moment, changed its position, then did this slow soft-step to the side, where I set two more down. Laurel and Bess were doing the same, with their usual self-assurance, I thought, until I noticed Bess's hand trembling as she worked on the pattern she was building.

"What are they doing?" I heard someone snap.

It was a woman's voice—imperious and sharp. It had to be the queen.

Another voice murmured something apologetic that I couldn't make out.

"Well, find out," the queen demanded.

I saw a footman approach Laurel. He poked her in the back with the end of his bow.

"You there," he said. "What are you doing?"

Her humming faltered, then died, leaving Bess to do a harmony on her own until she, too, stopped. Laurel turned to look at the footman and gave him a sweet smile that only me being her sister let me know she was a hair's breadth away from blowing her top.

Don't, don't, I thought. Don't talk to them. Don't tell them what we're doing.

But she held it in, though I guess being Laurel, she just *had* to ad-lib some.

"Cabbages need their kings, too," she said, then went back to what she was doing.

"What is *that* supposed to mean?" the queen shouted.

The footman poked Laurel again, but this time she completely ignored him. He turned his attention to me.

"You heard our queen," he said.

I thought I was ready for his poke, but I was in the middle of bending down and it made me lose my balance all the same. I went down on one shaking knee, expecting him to hit me or shoot me or I don't know what, but I made a point of laying out two more blades of grass, carefully arranging them, before getting back to my feet again.

"This is a trick of some kind," the queen said.

Of course it was. And it seemed that some others in the court thought the same, from the glimpses I snatched of them. But I could also see that the Apple Tree Man had been right: They were thoroughly mesmerized by what we were doing, trying to figure it all out.

"Just shoot one of them," the queen ordered.

I forgot to breathe then. The twitch between my

shoulder blades intensified. I knew the 'sangmen were ready to come charging out of the woods to help us, but at least one of us would die before they could do anything.

The fat little man who'd been standing with Ruth and Grace returned to my mind's eye.

The way the arrow flew into his throat.

The blood.

Seconds slipped by and I dared a glance at the bee fairies, quickly laying another blade of grass as I did. None of them had an arrow notched. They'd just come closer, trying to get a better look at what we were doing.

"You!" the queen cried to one of the footmen near me. "Shoot her."

But the footman was paying rapt attention to us, rather than her.

I did another dancey side step, even though Laurel and Bess weren't humming their tune anymore, and carefully laid down three more blades of grass in a triangular pattern.

The queen shouted at another of her footmen, and then at one of the riders who had dismounted to come closer. They both stared at our grass patterns and ignored her.

"Then I'll do it myself," the queen said.

She stepped to the footman standing closest to her and reached for his bow.

But before the queen could grab the bow, there came this god-awful cry from the woods where we'd left the 'sangmen. Anybody lives in these hills for a time knows that sound. It's the scream of a panther. You don't see them much at all, but time to time you'll hear that terrible cry of theirs, like a woman or child wailing in pain.

The cry was repeated, this time followed by a weird *pat-pat-pat* sound that seemed loud in the sudden stillness. I tried to figure out what it was. Then I remembered Aunt Lillian's stories about the Father of Cats and the sound his tail made as it slapped the ground.

The sound stopped everybody in their tracks, including the queen.

"The Father of Cats," I heard one of the fairies closest to me say in awe.

The queen shook off her paralysis and reached for the bow again, but the footman stepped back, pulling it out of her reach.

"I...I'm sorry, madam," he said. "But the Father of Cats has spoken."

I figured for sure she'd blow her stack at that. Instead, she sighed and walked over to where I continued my strange ritual of laying grass patterns.

"Very well," she said, blocking my way. "Let's end this nonsense, child. Tell me what you're doing and I'll give you the gift of your sisters' lives."

I ignored her, just as the Apple Tree Man had told me to, though I was surely tempted. But getting away from the bee fairies this one time wasn't enough. What was to stop them from coming after us again?

"You want more?" the queen asked. "What? Treasure? A long life? Good luck in love? A cure for your miserable freckles?"

I laid blades of grass at her feet, making a shape that started by her toe and then moved away till it looked like a fan.

"Answer me," the queen said.

I started to hum "Shenandoah," but I never could hold much of a tune. Luckily, first Bess, then Laurel picked it up, replacing my weak voice with their strong harmonies. I moved away from the queen to lay down more grass.

"Child," the queen said, her voice hard.

I took a pebble from my pocket and laid it on the ground, then balanced a blade of grass upon it.

"Offer her a boon," one of the other fairies said.

"Why should I? Perhaps I'll change her into a toad," the queen replied. "We'll see how well she dances and sings and lays down those ridiculous blades of grass then."

Could she even do that? Probably. She was magic, after all.

I heard a higher-pitched buzzing and saw that some of the bee fairies were tinier than I thought possible. I'd never noticed them before, though I had noticed the bees they were riding. I just hadn't realized there were little people on them until some flew right under my nose, trying to get a closer look at what I was doing.

"Offer her a boon," either the same bee fairy or another repeated.

"A boon, a boon," more of them took up, their little voices echoing across the meadow.

The queen said nothing for such a long time that I finally had to sneak a peek at her.

"Well, child?" she said. "Is that what it will take to unravel this mystery for us?"

I laid down one more blade of grass, then straightened up until I was facing her. She stood a full head taller than me, imperious and threatening. I gave a quick nod.

"Then ask your boon," she said. "But remember this: If you've played us for fools, if all this game of dancing and blades of grass is only so much nonsense, the bargain will be undone."

I let the last of my grass fall to the ground and clasped my hands in front of me.

"What are the limits of the boon you will grant?" I asked, repeating what the Apple Tree Man had told me to say when it came to this moment.

The queen's eyes narrowed and I knew that she realized I'd been coached, but there wasn't much she could do about it at this point.

"No harm can come to us or any under our protection," she said—reluctantly, it seemed.

It was pretty much the answer that the Apple Tree Man told us she'd have to give.

"Nothing else?" I asked.

"Nothing else."

"Then this is the boon I ask," I said. "That you

harm no one here, nor in any way cause harm to another for the rest of your days."

Fury raged in the queen's eyes now. The Apple Tree Man had warned us about that as well. She squeezed her fists and clenched her jaw, but finally she sighed heavily and gave an unwilling nod.

"The boon is granted," she said, her voice tight. "Now tell us what you were doing."

"A spell."

"That was no spell."

The Apple Tree Man had expected this as well.

I shrugged. "We were told it was a spell. We were told that only music and dancing and the pattern of the grass would rescue my sisters from you."

"Who told you this?"

"It doesn't matter," I said, though it clearly mattered plenty to her.

I beckoned to Ruth and Grace then. Laurel called out to Elsie. Just as I was about to ask after Adie, she came out of the trees behind the fairy court's horses, carrying a spear. She must have been planning to make her own try at a rescue.

"It's time you were going," I told the bee queen.

She shook her head. "No. You didn't play fair."

She made a swift gesture with her hand, and suddenly we were all gone from that field by Aunt Lillian's orchard and back in the Otherworld again.

"You lied about what you were doing."

"No, we—"

"Kill them!" the queen cried. "Kill them all. Then go back into their world and kill their mother. Kill all their friends and their friends' families. Burn down their homes. Salt their fields."

There was a maniacal look in the bee queen's eyes, but I suppose it didn't much matter. Crazy or not, she was the queen and there was nothing we could do to stop her—not with only the seven of us and the fairy court in this world, and our 'sangmen friends left behind in the other.

Looked like I was right, always to be so scared of bees. Some part of me must have known that one day they'd kill me.

I saw Adie raise her spear. I stepped in front of Ruth and Grace. Laurel and Bess came to stand beside me, though what the three of us could do to protect the younger twins, I didn't know. Elsie was halfway from the tree where she'd been standing to where we were. She stopped dead with bee fairies all around her.

An ugly murmur went through the court. The bees carrying the tiny fairies buzzed angrily in the air all around us. All I wanted to do was close my eyes and have it over with, but I couldn't. I had to go down swatting them bees, doing what I could to keep my sisters as safe as I could before the bees finally brought me down.

Turned out it wasn't necessary.

Those bee fairies weren't mad at us. They were mad at their queen.

One of the tall riders stepped up to her, and before she could stop him, he grabbed hold of a pendant she was wearing and gave it a sharp tug. The chain broke and he stepped back with the pendant in his hand just before she took a swing at him. Before she could try again, he pointed a finger at her.

"Enough. We've put up with your anger and feuds for too long as it is," he said. "But when you break a solemn oath, you go too far."

The queen fixed him with a cold look. "Don't you *dare* judge me. I am your queen and so long as I—"

"Queen no longer," he broke in.

He lifted a hand and those bee-riding fairies came swarming. There were thousands, I figure. Each with a bow and a quiver filled with tiny venomed arrows.

"When you broke your oath," he said, "you forfeited your royalty. You have no place in this court."

He cut downward with his hand and all those little bee fairies let loose with their arrows.

I didn't much like that queen. Truth be told, the way she threatened me and my sisters, I wouldn't have cried to find out she'd up and died somewhere, somehow. But to see her killed, right there in front of my eyes, all I felt was sick.

She dropped to the ground with all those little arrows sticking out of her like she was a pincushion, screaming and writhing from the pain of the venom. I began to step forward, wanting to do something to ease her pain, but Bess caught hold of my arm.

"Wait," the bee fairy who'd given the order to have her killed said to me.

The queen stopped screaming, her movements slowing as she lay there on the grass.

The bees carrying the tiny archers had all landed now, most on the ground, some on the foliage nearby.

It was so quiet in the meadow that the queen's dying gasp echoed for what seemed like forever.

I looked at the new leader of the fairy court.

"Wait," he repeated.

And then I heard it—the same sound I'd heard in the Apple Tree Man's house. The rumbling drone of a bee swarm coming from inside the dead queen. My sisters on either side gasped as the newborn bees came swarming up out of the queen's mouth.

There were a lot of them—far more than had come out of the little 'sangman. So many that, for a long moment, we couldn't even see the bee queen. Then they went spiraling up and away, this dark buzzing swarm of bees, like a storm cloud driven afore the wind. All that was left of the queen was the shape of her, made up of what looked like old, dried honeycombs, all gray and papery.

The new leader looked like he was about to say something to me, but just then we heard a commotion at the far end of the court. The bees' dogs started up barking as out of the woods came an army of 'sangmen, led by their king and queen. The 'sangman I'd rescued walked beside them, hand-in-hand with the last daughter of the bee queen. In among the crowd of 'sangmen I spied Aunt Lillian, the Apple Tree Man, and Li'l Pater, who, I found out later, was the one who'd brought them all over to this part of the Otherworld.

"Hold!" the leader of the bee fairies cried to the court as they started notching arrows and aiming spears.

He walked through the court to meet the 'sangmen. After glancing at one another, my sisters and I trailed along behind him, Adie and Elsie joining us so that all seven of us were together. The 'sangmen awaited the bee fairy's approach. They were purely outnumbered, no question about it, but they looked ready to fight all the same.

But the fight never happened. The bee man went down on one knee in front of the princess and offered her the pendant that he'd torn from her mother's neck. She hesitated for a long moment, then accepted it. The court erupted into cheers, all the bee fairies grinning at one another, gone in the blink of an eye from grim, dangerous creatures to folks just looking for an excuse to have a party.

My sisters and I exchanged puzzled looks, but I was feeling hopeful that all our troubles were done.

The princess—I guess I should call her the queen now—signaled the bee man to rise, then had him lead her to us. There was a merry laugh in her eyes, but when she spoke, it was serious, like a ceremony.

"Your boon was fairly asked and just," she said. "We have no quarrel with you, nor with any other. Will you promise us the same?"

"Well, sure," I said. "We never wanted any trouble in the first place."

She sighed. "So it would appear. My mother... she..."

"Wasn't exactly easy to get along with."

She nodded.

"Still," I said, "it was harsh, what happened to her."

When she gave me a puzzled look, I added, "You know, killing her and all. If it were my mama..." I didn't finish. Our situations were too different to compare.

"Did your mother lock you in a tower for most of your life?" she asked. "Did she never have a kind word for you?"

"I'm sorry," I said. "You don't have to explain. I know things were different for you."

She gave a slow nod. "They were." She waited a beat, then added, "But she wasn't killed. She was changed into a new tribe. This is her chance to begin again and make amends for the wrongs she did in this life."

That all sounded fine and dandy, but it put a big question in my head. I didn't know quite how to ask, but I had to know.

"Is there...any chance she could get it into her head to come after us again?" I asked.

"No. You'll be safe now. You and your sisters and anyone under your protection. You have my word on that."

"Thanks for that," I said.

"No. Thank you," she said. "All of you," she added, looking around to take in my sisters and the 'sangmen as well.

She held out her hand and the little 'sangman prince left his parents' side to come and stand by her.

"We both thank you," she said.

There was a moment's silence, then the fairy court cheered again. This time the 'sangmen joined in.

I guess this is where most fairy tales would end. Trouble was, we still had to get home.

"id you hear me roar like the Father of Cats?" Li'l Pater asked me.

"That was you?"

He nodded, then whapped his tail on the ground to make that *pat-pat-pat* sound we'd heard after the panther's scream.

"Guess you saved the day," I told him.

"Bet you're glad I came along now."

"Better than glad," I said, and I meant it.

Both fairy courts had departed and we were alone in the meadow now, just Aunt Lillian and us Dillard girls, the Apple Tree Man, and Li'l Pater. My sisters didn't know what to make of this pair of fairy people, but they were taking it in good stride. I suppose with everything they'd already seen today, spending time with a little cat man and a fellow who looked more like a tree than a man was pretty tame. Heck, Grace and Ruth were already tussling in the grass with Li'l Pater like he was some long-lost friend, paying no mind to the rest of us.

But while I was grateful for the help the pair of them had given us, I was pretty much done with fairy-lands and the people in them. I went over to where the Apple Tree Man and Aunt Lillian were talking.

"I want to go home," I told him. "I purely hate it here."

"Of course," the Apple Tree Man said. "But you know, you've only seen the worst this place has to offer. There is far more laughter and glory in this land than could ever be represented by feuding fairy courts."

What happened to how dangerous it was for or-dinary folks to cross over here? I wondered. But I didn't press him on it. I got the sense he wasn't talk-ing to me anyway, but to Aunt Lillian. I don't know why I didn't see this coming, but as soon as she put her hand on his arm I knew that she'd be staying.

"I won't be coming back," she said.

"I guess I knew that," I said, "but that doesn't make it any easier."

"I know. But I've got a chance here...." She shot a glance at the Apple Tree Man and I had to smile. "I guess I just need to take it."

I didn't know what to say. It wasn't my place to steal this moment of happiness, but I was going to miss her something terrible.

"I made arrangements sometime back with my lawyer," she went on, "for everything to go to you. I was thinking of it as an inheritance, but now...I suppose it's a gift. You're the only one I know who will take care of all I hold dear. I just have to come back and stop by his office to sign it over to you and make it official."

Now I really didn't know what to say.

"What?" Laurel asked. "You mean you're giving her that ramshackle old homestead?"

Bess elbowed her in the side.

"Sorry," Laurel muttered.

But Aunt Lillian didn't take offense.

"The homestead," she said. "Yes. But also the hills. I can't recall exactly how much land's involved.

Something in the neighborhood of a hundred square miles, I reckon. The lawyer will know for sure."

"You own all that land behind our farm?" Adie asked.

"No one *really* owns the land," Aunt Lillian told her. "But I guess I hold the paper on it."

"But you..."

Aunt Lillian grinned. "Live plain and simple and poor as a church mouse?"

"Something like that."

"Maybe she doesn't have any money," Elsie said, a smug look on her face. "But I'm guessing Lily McGlure has more than enough."

"Who's Lily McGlure?" Laurel asked.

"Famous artist," Adie told her. "Loads of money."

I wondered how Adie'd come to know something like that, but it got explained pretty quick.

"I'm sorry," Elsie was saying to Aunt Lillian. "I know we shouldn't have looked in that chest with all your paintings and sketchbooks, but we got scared when we couldn't find you or Janey. So then we got thinking about bodies and where you could hide them..."

"That's all right, girl," Aunt Lillian said. "It's

nothing I'm ashamed of. I just always kept my distance from being Lily McGlure on account of once folks know you've got money, they come hounding you for it and you never do get no peace. Folks always knew me as Lily Kindred, living with her aunt, Em Kindred, though I was indeed born Lillian Mc-Glure. It was purely a girlish whim I took to use the McGlure name on my art at first, but later I saw the advantage of it and, well, I just left it that way."

"You're a famous artist?" I asked. "When did that happen?"

"Oh, a long time ago," Aunt Lillian said. "I started in on drawing when I was younger than you and I guess I did pretty well because, after a time, I had me all these folks in Newford, and even farther off, falling over themselves to buy what I was doing. Got me an agent and everything, selling both the originals as well as prints and the like. Aunt Em and me, well, we didn't need more than we had—and didn't want it, neither. So first off, I bought all this land to keep it safe from the mining and logging companies and such, and then I had any other money coming my way put into a trust fund to take care of taxes and all.

"A body could get themselves proper rich, selling

off the land and using the money in that fund, I reckon."

"I would never do that," I told her.

She smiled. "I know. Why do you think I'm leaving it to you, girl? But you ever find you need some money, maybe to get you an education, or for one of your sisters, don't you be shy about selling off some of that old artwork of mine. And you'll find a treat or two, down at the bottom of that chest. I got me three color studies by Milo Johnson, any one of which'd fetch top dollar at an auction."

Elsie's eyes went wide, but the rest of us didn't much know who she was talking about.

"Probably another famous artist," Laurel said.

"Only the most famous to paint in these hills," Elsie said, "after Lily McGlure."

"Now you're embarrassing me, girl," Aunt Lillian said, but I could see she was pleased with the compliment all the same.

"Why did you stop painting?" Elsie asked.

Aunt Lillian shrugged. "I don't know. I got old and my fingers got stiff. And I said pretty much all I had to say with my paints, I reckon, though I've still been drawing in one of my sketchbooks from time to time. The thing is, you do a thing long enough, don't matter how much you love it, it can start to wear some and you want to turn to something else. Gets so you look at what could be the perfect picture and you just want to hold it in your head and appreciate it for what it is, 'stead of trying to capture it on canvas.

"And after Aunt Em died, I didn't really have the time no more."

She turned to me.

"You remember this, girl," she said. "You don't have to be no spinster to live out on that old homestead and do it right."

I just shrugged.

"There's just one more thing," Aunt Lillian said. "I'm leaving you with a lot of benefits, I guess, though truth to tell, it just lets my heart rest easy knowing that everything I got's passing into such good and capable hands. But I've got to leave you with an unpaid debt as well."

"What's that?"

"Well, that Father of Cats that Li'l Pater and the fairies were talking about—that's the same old black panther in those stories I told you 'bout from when I was a girl. You 'member them?"

I gave a slow nod.

"Well then, I reckon you remember how I owe him. That debt's supposed to pass on to my children and their children after. But I never had me a child. I guess the closest I've come is you, so I'm asking you to take that on as well."

"What...what's he going to ask me to do?"

I knew I couldn't say no to Aunt Lillian, but I was remembering how even those fierce bee fairies had seemed wary when they thought the Father of Cats was taking an interest in their affairs. And if he scared *them*...

"I don't rightly know," Aunt Lillian said. "But I told him I'd only do whatever it was if no one would be hurt by it."

"The Father of Cats is an honorable being," the Apple Tree Man said. "What he asks of you might be hard, but it won't be wrong."

I nodded. "Okay," I said. "I'll take on that debt for you, Aunt Lillian." I turned to the Apple Tree Man, adding, "And I guess I owe you an apology, just like I did Li'l Pater. I should have just trusted you."

He smiled. "Nothing wrong with someone need- ing to earn your trust. I'm just happy it all worked out the way it did. You were very brave out there with the bee fairies."

"I didn't feel brave. I just felt stupid."

"Oh, I know," Bess said. "And scared, too. I was sure they'd hear my knees knocking against each other from one end of the meadow to the other."

I looked at her for a long moment.

"But you and Laurel," I finally said. "You're always doing stuff in front of people. Playing and singing and dancing."

"Well, I get nervous doing that sometimes, too," Bess said. "Laurel's the one who's not scared of anything."

Laurel laughed. "What's the worst that can happen? You make a fool of yourself, but life goes on."

"Except here we could've gotten ourselves shot like the queen did," I said.

Laurel went quiet pretty fast.

"There's that," she said.

I turned back to the Apple Tree Man.

"It's time we were going," I said.

I'd told the truth before, about not wanting to be in this place. But right now I didn't want to go, because it meant leaving Aunt Lillian behind. I figured

I'd probably see her from time to time, but nothing was going to be the same anymore. I was happy to look after that place of hers for her, but I was also thinking how that could be a lonely way to live, especially with her being gone and all.

I guess she knew what I was thinking. She came up and put her arms around me and just held me for a time.

"You'll do fine, girl," she said.

I held on tight to her for a moment longer, then we gathered up Grace and Ruth from across the meadow, where they were playing leapfrog with Li'l Pater, and we all made our way back to where the door into the Apple Tree Man's house opened out on this world.

guess Root pretty much thought he'd died and gone to heaven when me and all my sisters came traipsing out of the Apple Tree Man's tree. He jumped up and barked and ran around in circles, not knowing who to greet first. But he finally settled on me, stood up, and put his paws on my stomach, looking at me like I was the best thing he could ever find in this world, which, I suppose, from his point of view I was, seeing's how I'm the one that first found him and does most of the looking after for him. But he was a dog full of love, and after I'd fussed some with him, he went and visited everybody else, full of wet kisses, that tail of his wagging so hard you'd think it was going to come off.

"Well, some things don't change," Adie said as she took Root's paws in her hands and pushed him away from her. "I swear that dog's got double his quota of loving enthusiasm."

"He just missed us," Ruth said, bending down and not minding Root's sloppy kisses all over her face.

Adie pulled her to her feet.

"Don't let him do that," she said. "He's putting germs all over your face."

"Is that true?" Ruth asked Elsie, the Dillard expert in all things natural.

Elsie shrugged. "Probably."

"Just think where that tongue of his has been," Adie said.

"Yeah," Laurel put in. "You forget what he uses to lick his butt?"

Seemed we were already settling right back into our usual sisterly ways.

"Anybody know what time it is?" Adie asked.

None of us had a watch, but I checked the position of the sun.

"Four," I said. "Maybe four thirty."

"We should get a move on," Adie said. "Mama's going to kill us, and don't think for a minute she's going to buy the story of what really happened to us today."

"Hang on," I said. "I just need to get Henny back into the barn and feed the chickens."

"We'll help," Grace and Ruth chorused in the same breath.

"And let's have one more look in that chest of Aunt Lillian's," Elsie said.

Adie started to shake her head, but as soon as Elsie brought it up, we were all interested.

"What's another half hour," Bess asked, "when we're already as late as we are?"

"Yeah," Laurel said to Adie. "You've already had a peek at all those pictures of hers."

I don't suppose Adie had much choice in the matter, not with all of us determined. Laurel and Elsie rounded up Henny and put her back into the barn, milking her and making sure that she had water and feed, while the younger twins and I saw to the chickens. We threw down extra feed for them, in case I was late getting back up tomorrow. Then we all trooped into the house and up the stairs to the second floor.

I guess with Aunt Lillian having been this famous artist, I should have expected her work to be good, but I was still right surprised when I got an actual look at all those fine drawings and paintings that filled the chest.

"They're not paintings," Elsie explained, when Laurel wondered aloud why the wooden panels Aunt Lillian had used weren't hanging in some museum. "They're what you call studies, something you do in preparation for the real painting."

Ruth picked one up and held it closer to her face. "They look like real paintings to me."

"Sure do," Grace said. "They look good enough to hang in a museum to me." She turned to her twin. "Remember that school trip we took to the museum in Tyson? These pictures are better than half the stuff we saw in there."

Ruth nodded. "Yeah, at least these are about something."

"Any museum would pay top dollar to own these," Elsie said.

Laurel grinned. "I guess that means you're rich, Janey."

"Only if she sells them," Elsie reminded us. "She might not want to do that."

"I've got to think on it," I said.

Truth was, I was feeling a little overwhelmed. It was strange enough, knowing I'd be holding paper on the homestead and all the hills around us, without taking into account all these paintings and sketchbooks. What I really wanted was to have Aunt Lillian back and for things to be the way they'd been before. I already missed her something terrible.

"You could probably afford to put in electricity and a phone line," Adie said.

Laurel laughed. "Why's she got to do that? She can just buy herself a big old house in town—have cable and everything."

"That's not the point," I said.

Adie shook her head. "So what is? To live hard and never have the time to enjoy life a little?"

"I don't know that it's something I can explain," I said. "I felt the same way as you do when I first came up here and saw how Aunt Lillian was living. But the more I helped out and the more I learned, the more I came to understand that easy's not necessarily better. When you do pretty much everything for yourself, you appreciate the things you've got a lot more than if someone just up and hands it to you, or you buy it off the shelf in some store."

Adie looked at me for a long moment and I knew she still didn't get it. But she wasn't going to argue with me, neither.

"We should go," she said. "Mama's going to be back by now and worried sick."

I nodded in agreement and was ready to leave, but just then Elsie pulled some more paintings from the bottom of the chest.

"Here they are," she said.

"Are these paintings or—what did you call them—studies?" Ruth wanted to know.

"They were done as studies, the same as those of Aunt Lillian, but I guess they're paintings, too."

There were three of them and even I could tell right off that they'd been done by somebody else.

The first was of the staircase waterfall, where the creek took a sudden tumble before heading on again at a quieter pace. The second was of that old deserted homestead up a side valley of the hollow, its tin roof sagging, rotting walls falling inward. The last one could have been painted anywhere in this forest, but it was easy to imagine it had been done down by the creek, looking up the slope into a view of yellow birches, beech, and sprucy-pines growing thick and dense, with a shaft of light coming through a break in the canopy.

I don't know much about art, but I liked these paintings a lot. They were kind of rough—without much detail—but I could recognize where they'd been done, and they were about as good as a picture gets. Not better than Aunt Lillian's, just different. But Elsie got more excited than I'd seen her in a long time.

"These are the ones by Milo Johnson," she said.

"The other famous artist," Adie said. "One of the two fellows who disappeared in these woods back in the twenties or something that you were telling me about."

Elsie nodded. "And now we know where they ended up."

None of us said much for a time. We just sat there by the chest, thinking about the day we'd had.

"Any of you got a bad urge to go back across?" I asked.

Adie and the older twins shook their heads. The younger twins looked primed and ready, but I think that had more to do with the fun they'd had with Li'l Pater. Only Elsie got this kind of dreamy look that put a deep worry in me.

"Say you won't try to go back," I said to her.

She blinked, then looked at me. "I don't know. Everything was so much more *there* than it is here. I hated all the business with those fairy courts, but I've got to admit that if the chance came up, I'd probably go."

"Promise me you won't unless you talk to me first."

She met my gaze, then gave a slow nod.

"Okay, I promise," she said.

"We have *got* to go home," Adie said.

We put everything back into the chest, except for one of the sketchbooks filled with drawings and little handwritten descriptions of various plants and such. I wanted to bring it home with me, so I put it in the backpack that Adie'd used to carry preserves for Aunt Lillian. Then I closed the door to her house—no, it's my house now, I realized—and we headed for home, stopping only to collect Laurel's and Bess's instrument cases along the way.

Grace and Ruth played innocent, but it didn't take us long to figure out who'd played that trick of filling those cases with stones. I guess the only thing that saved them from getting a licking from the older twins was how close we'd all come to dying. Thing like that puts everything into a different perspective, that's for sure.

here was a thunderstorm in Mama's eyes when we came trailing out of the woods and crossed the pasture to home. She didn't even acknowledge Root's happy greeting, just stood there with her hands on her hips as we came up to her.

"Now remember," Adie had warned when we were on the path coming home. "We lost track of time and we'll just accept whatever Mama gives us in punishment. No talk about fairy courts and Otherworlds or we'll all be looking at a licking."

Everybody'd agreed with her, though none of us felt real happy about the prospect of telling Mama such a big lie. Plus we still had to figure out a way to explain how Aunt Lillian had come to go away and leave all her property and lands to me.

But agreeing's one thing, doing's another, and Ruth and Grace were just too excited by it all to remember to keep it to themselves.

"Mama! Mama!" Grace cried as she broke from us and ran toward her. "You're not going to believe the story we have to tell you."

For as Long a Time
as Distance

CHAPTER TWENTY-SIX

Sarah Jane

I was splitting wood and putting it up in the woodshed for the winter when Root gave a warning bark. I set down the ax and turned to see what had caught his attention. With Root it could be anything from crows in the corn to a groundhog getting too bold for his britches— just saying a groundhog wore britches.

For a second I didn't see anything. Then this fellow came out of the woods on the far side of the trees, moving so smooth and easy it was like he'd just appeared there. I had a moment's worry, thinking maybe this was some more business with the fairies, but as he got closer, I could see he was human. Leastwise he looked human, though handsomer than most boys I've run across.

He was wearing hiking boots, jeans, and a white T-shirt with a buckskin jacket overtop, and carrying an ax. His hair was black as a starless night under a baseball cap turned backward. His broad features had a coppery cast to them, so I figured he was probably from the rez. Even with that jacket on you could tell he was strong as well as graceful.

"Hey," he said. "Is Lily around?"

My mouth felt too dry to talk, so I just shook my head.

He smiled. "I see you're doing my job."

"Your...job?" I managed.

"Putting in the winter wood."

He held out a hand so that Root could give it a sniff, then bent and ruffled his fur. Standing up again, he came over and offered me his hand, too—to shake, not smell.

"I'm Oliver," he said. "Oliver Creek."

"Sarah Jane Dillard."

His palm was dry and a little rough, and my pulse just started going quicker. I let go of his hand and took a step back. I didn't know what was the matter with me. I was feeling so hot I figured I must have a fever.

"Are you always this quiet, Sarah Jane?" he asked.

I shook my head.

"My granddad's a friend of Lily's," he went on. "We help her out with some of the heavier work around here."

"Like chopping wood."

He held up his ax and nodded. "You want a hand?"

"Sure. Thanks."

We didn't talk much as we worked. Oliver was better at chopping and splitting than I was, so I let him go to it and spent most of my time stacking the stove lengths in the woodshed. After a couple of hours, we took a break and sat on stumps by the woodpile, sipping iced tea.

"So where's Lily?" Oliver asked. "Out hunting and gathering?"

I smiled and shook my head. "She's...gone away."

He gave me a sharp look, and I realized what that had sounded like.

"No, she's not dead or anything," I quickly said. "She's just moved...." I sighed. "It's complicated."

"She's gone into the Otherworld," Oliver said.

Now it was my turn to look hard at him.

"You know about all of that?" I asked.

He shrugged. "My mother's got sixteen sisters and they're all medicine women, so all I've ever heard

since I was a kid was about the *manitou* and *manidò-akì*—
the spiritworld. Never been there myself, though.
Never seen a spirit, either, but I guess I believe they're
out there."

"So what makes you think Aunt Lillian went over
there?"

"Well, Granddad's told me about this friendship
she's got with some tree spirit in the orchard and how
every time he used to come up here he'd half expect
her to have gone off into *manidò-akì* with him."

"John Creek," I said. "That's who your grandfather
is, right?"

It was coming back to me now.

He smiled. "That's right. And I'm still Oliver."

"Aunt Lillian's told me about you."

"All good, I hope."

I don't know why it came over me, but I had to
duck my head to hide a blush.

"Well, that's where she went," I said, hiding behind my hair and pretending to look at something on
the ground. "Into that Otherworld with the Apple
Tree Man."

"She leave the place in your care?"

I nodded.

"So you mind if I come by from time to time?" he asked.

I looked up at him. "You don't have to. I'm not as old as Aunt Lillian—at least not yet. I can do the heavy work."

"I wasn't offering to do work," he said, "though I'm happy to lend a hand. I was thinking more of just coming by to visit."

"Why would you want to do that?"

I don't know why that came out the way it did. I was just too nervous, I guess. And now I figured I'd just insulted him or something. But he only smiled.

"Because I like you, Sarah Jane," he said. "And I'd like to get to know you better."

He got up then and fetched his ax from where he'd stuck it in the chopping stump.

"I've got to go," he said. "I promised Granddad I'd come by and give him a hand mending his traps before it got dark."

I stood up and didn't know what to do with my hands.

"Thanks for all your help," I said. "I would've been at this all day if you hadn't come by."

"No problem. You busy tomorrow?"

I thought about a hundred things I still had to do, from chores to getting the place ready for winter, and almost said so when I realized what he was really asking.

"No," I said, and then I got real brave. "Would you like to come for dinner?"

"I'll count the minutes," he said with a grin.

He gave Root a quick pat, tapped his index finger against his temple, and pointed it at me, then headed off, back across the field. I just stood there watching him go until he disappeared among the trees, then sat back down on the stump and hugged my knees.

"You hear that, Root?" I said. "He said he liked me."

⌀

So I guess that's my story.

If you want to know more about Aunt Lillian and the Apple Tree Man, or if the Father of Cats ever came to see me, or even what kind of mischief Ruth and Grace got into with Li'l Pater—those are all stories for another time.

Anything else...well, it's nobody's business but my own.

CHARLES DE LINT is the much-beloved author of more than seventy adult, young adult, and children's books, including *The Cats of Tanglewood Forest*, *Seven Wild Sisters*, *The Blue Girl*, *The Painted Boy*, and *Under My Skin*. Well-known throughout fantasy and science-fiction circles as one of the trailblazers of the modern fantasy genre, he is the recipient of the World Fantasy, White Pine, Crawford, and Aurora Awards. De Lint is a poet, songwriter, performer, and folklorist, and he writes a monthly book-review column for the *Magazine of Fantasy & Science Fiction*. He shares his home in Ottawa, Canada, with his wife, MaryAnn Harris.

CHARLES VESS is a world-renowned artist and a three-time winner of the World Fantasy Award, among several others. His work has appeared in magazines, comic books, and novels, including *The Cats of Tanglewood Forest*; *Seven Wild Sisters*; *The Coyote Road—Trickster Tales*; *Peter Pan*; *The Book of Ballads*; and *Stardust*, written by Neil Gaiman and made into an acclaimed film by Paramount Pictures. Vess has also illustrated two picture books with Gaiman (*Instructions* and *Blueberry Girl*) that were *New York Times* bestsellers. His art has been featured in several gallery and museum exhibitions around the world. He lives in southwest Virginia.

Artist's Note

Most of the illustrations in this book were originally created as black-and-white pen-and-ink drawings for a limited edition of *Seven Wild Sisters* published many years ago. For this current edition, my publisher asked me to refresh those drawings with color. But because the original art had long since been sold, I only had access to digital scans. Using an Adobe Photoshop program, I transformed my complex weave of fine black lines into sepia tones more suited to my application of color. Then, after printing the images on Arches watercolor paper, I applied layer after layer of colored FW Inks.

For the twenty-six illustrations that are new to this edition, I first worked them up in pencil, this time on Strathmore (4 ply) 500 Bristol paper, and then hatched a handmade sepia-toned ink over them using a Hunt Crow Quill 102 nib. In order to give these pieces the same density of line as the original set of illustrations, I momentarily pretended that they would be published only in black and white. Afterward, I erased any loose pencil lines and applied my colors. Can you tell which pieces are new and which ones are old?

—Charles Vess

About This Book

This book was edited by Andrea Spooner and Deirdre Jones and designed by Saho Fujii under the art direction of Dave Caplan and Sasha Illingworth. The production was supervised by Virginia Lawther, and the production editor was Christine Ma. This book was printed on 100-gsm Gold Sun Woodfree paper. The text was set in MrsEaves, and the display type is hand-lettered.